Creepy Campfire Stories
(for Grownups)

**Edited by
Jennifer Word**

EMP Publishing

Creepy Campfire Stories (for Grownups)
Compilation Copyright © 2015 EMP Publishing

DEDICATION

*To the memory of every creepy tale told 'round the campfire –
and those who told it – since the dawn of humanity.*

CONTENTS

ACKNOWLEDGMENTS

A huge thank you is necessary to a multitude of people. First and foremost, a giant heap of gratitude goes to the associate editors, Kimberly King and Theresa Huffman, who tirelessly waded through hundreds of submissions for this anthology.

This book also would not have been possible without the support and encouragement of the following:

A.C. Powell, Cassandra Wolff, J. Hall, Richard French, Linda L. French, Ereika Stimley, Jenny Koenig, Edward Ahern, Christopher Couch, Dave Thorn, Nacreous, P.V. Limbaugh, Paul M. Feeney, Gerard Huntman, Russell McGuigan, Darryl D. Brown, Kimberly King, Matt Andrew, Lisa M. Lorelli, Justin Smith, Theresa Huffman, Dale A. Russell, Andrea Baskir, Aden Routly, Brendan Prost, Tamara Fey Turner, Adrian Ludens, C. Willis, Alan H. Fine, H. Sanchez, J. Togando, Clara Saenz.

INTRODUCTION

I was born and raised in Anchorage, Alaska. From a very young age, my parents would take advantage of the very short summer season every year, from roughly the first of June through September, to bask in the beauty and glory of the Alaskan wilderness in summertime. I have countless memories of sleeping in tents (and sleeping bags), motorhomes, and even onboard boats in foggy Southern Alaskan harbors and marinas (shout out to Soldotna and Homer) during my families' various camping excursions and adventures. We even spent an entire month, one glorious summer, exploring just over the border. I've panned for gold in the Yukon, visited the cabin of poet Robert Service in Dawson City, and come face-to-face on countless occasions with moose, most of them in my own front yard. And every summer, no matter what form of camping we did, there was always a beach, or river, and freshly caught fish fried up in pans (or hot dogs, if short of a catch), followed by toasted marshmallows on stripped, green and sappy birch sticks from the forest floor, and the impending scary campfire tale.

These wonderful summertime memories are only complete in my mind because of every detail, always included, not least of which was the scary story told around the flames, with the ever-changing Alaskan breeze inevitably blowing smoke into my eyes. No camping or adventure day was ever perfect or complete without that spooky tale right at the very end. And I believe it was those creepy campfire yarns that first planted the seed in my young mind for the love and appreciation of stories in general. I learned to love stories long before I even knew how to read. But I always loved the scary ones the most.

There's just something about a creepy campfire story, told in the dark, with only the glow of the fire to see by. The front of your body over-hot, the skin on your face feeling stretched, dry and crispy, yet, your back feeling icily cold, a wall of black behind you, and who-knows-what lurking in the woods, or just down the beach, where the firelight doesn't reach. Suddenly, even the silliest of monsters, or the most sloppily of told stories becomes the freakiest thing you've ever heard. The most outrageously unbelievable stories, in the darkness and isolation of the wilderness, become so credible, you believe the story is, or could, happen to you.

It has been quite a while since I last camped out in the woods, or roasted marshmallows around a campfire, enjoying horror stories that make my skin crawl. But that doesn't mean I can't still try to find a way to invoke similar feelings and experiences with the written word. I've carefully selected nineteen various stories, all of them creepy or dark in their own, unique fashion, that I hope will leave readers reaching to turn more lights on, or perhaps, jumping at every creak and groan of your home settling at night, or the wind blowing outside your window. The selection is myriad, as readers' tastes on what actually scares each one of us varies like those proverbial Alaskan breezes. However, I feel confident that no matter who you are, there're guaranteed to be at least a few stories in here that will invoke that campfire story feel of discomfort, disturbance, fear, or even euphoria.

Some of these stories are decently extreme. A few had me cringing, or even exclaiming out loud, "Oh my God!" and "Ew...". Let's see if you have any of the same reactions.

Of the authors whose stories were selected to fill this book, all I can relay there, is how absolutely impressed and astounded I was while reading their stories. I can honestly say that I believe this book is a perfect representation of the most talented, exemplary and cutting edge modern horror writers practicing their craft today. And they come from all over the world. Because scary stories should have no boundaries, and fear is a universal emotion.

So, sit back, relax, turn off the lights (save for one to read by) and enjoy these modern day creepy campfire stories. The universal element is simply fear, and ordinary people facing extraordinary circumstances. Whether the stories take place around an actual campfire in the woods, a typical suburban residence, or a prison, the predicaments of the characters is a

Introduction

bonding experience of compassion and relief that you aren't them. Whether the tales take place in modern times, in the past, or fantasy settings, the experiences of the characters inevitably become yours, so immerse yourself in these new, classic campfire stories, and remember...you're safe, so long as you don't look into the dark just behind you.

Welcome to the campfire...

Jennifer Word
August 5, 2015

DENYING THE THRILL
Gerry Huntman

Detective Superintendent Geoff Mitchell stormed into the interrogation room, shutting and locking the steel-reinforced door.

Shit. Geoff's crazy. Mark unconsciously tugged his handcuffed wrist, which was fastened to his heavy, steel chair. *We're alone. He's going to kill me.*

Mitchell kept his back to Mark. It was deliberate. The detective took several deep breaths; sweat glistened on his balding head.

"I changed the code to the locking system, Mark. I've got twenty minutes, minimum. No one can get in." The voice was controlled but there was a tsunami-rage building underneath.

"I didn't do it, Geoff. I swear it."

Geoff Mitchell spun around, lunged forward, slamming both his fists on the small table separating him and Mark. For a fifty-year-old, he was very strong. "You killed my daughter, you fucking bastard! I trusted you to look after her. You sliced her throat to the bone and let her bleed out like a fucking pig!" Spit sprayed everywhere, long trails bungeed from his lower lip and chin. His eyes were wide and bloodshot; face a brilliant pink.

"You've got to believe me. Just wait a while — your team will find evidence to prove I didn't do it."

"Bullshit! My baby's dead—" His face screwed into itself. "Slaughtered." He wailed, collapsing into an empty chair on his side of the table. "M...my baby is *dead*."

For the first time since he discovered Lily's body, Mark wept. Long, deep crying that heaved his chest in each wave.

"If you didn't do it, why aren't you angry? I'm angry. *Real* angry." Geoff locked his scarlet-lined, moist gaze on Mark's eyes for the first time.

"Believe me, I'm angry...*was* angry. You see...I saw this coming a long time ago."

***

Mark's return to his home city of Melbourne, Australia, after a ten-year break, coincided with his class reunion party. He stepped into the Richmond Function Centre with trepidation. *I hate this sort of shit.*

The hum of a hundred voices and the blaring strains of Nickelback flooded through an open doorway into the front foyer.

He stepped into strobing lights and a large hall full of clusters of people, chatting, laughing.

This is a mistake.

"Is that you, Mark?"

His eyes adjusted to the dim lighting, and ten years of aging of the woman before him. "Margot? Margot Fielding?"

"Yep! The one and only!"

"You organized this, didn't you?" Mark needed to get the conversation going. He loathed small talk but hated silence more.

"Sure did. I haven't changed much; remember, I was on our school council and social committee."

Mark smiled and surprised himself by not forcing it. "No, we never change much."

Margot introduced him to people he barely remembered and found the conversation so-so. Most of them had gone to college and found good jobs. A few were successful by anyone's definition. He didn't like talking about himself but when cornered, admitted he was a commercial artist — did some cool and funky stuff. Mark eased himself out of the groups on that cue each and every time — he never felt comfortable being in the spotlight. He was fast running out of groups to join, and reflected that it was an apt metaphor of his years at high school.

Mark slunk his way back to the foyer, ensuring he got his money's worth of bourbon down his gullet along the way. A slight woman stepped out of the shadows, intercepting his course.

She was pretty, with a cute, upturned nose.

"Don't you remember me?" she asked.

Memories flooded in. She was slightly heavier, and had shorter, darker hair. "Lily! Oh my God. It's Lily!" He held out his hand, resisting the impulse to hug her.

She warmly shook his hand. "I didn't expect you turning up, Mark. You were always the quiet type."

He laughed. "I was…am. I don't know why I came but I did. Suppose I live within walking distance."

"And you were about to leave."

"Um. Yeah. People don't change much." He found it difficult to keep eye contact with her. "It didn't occur to me you'd come. You left halfway through senior school without warning."

"Had to. Dad's a cop and he got a temporary transfer up north to Shepparton. We returned to Melbourne a few years later, but by then all my school friends had moved on."

"I…I missed you." He cursed himself as soon as he said it. This was a girl he had fallen in love with a long time ago. The beginnings of a relationship had been nurtured, and Lily was the first person in his life that he wanted to reveal his special secret to — his curse. She had then dropped off the planet.

Lily's eyebrows rose in surprise at his confession, and she smiled. "I missed you, too."

They left the reunion early. Together.

***

"Why haven't you asked me to shack up with you?" Lily asked. She snuggled against Mark's bare chest, running her fingers through his hair, entwining her legs with his beneath the bed sheet.

He sighed, feeling the weight of his curse—his secret— remaining unsaid for ten years, pressing on him. He so loved Lily, and the past few months confirmed what he knew was real when he was a teenager.

"What's wrong? Don't you want to take the next step?" Lily's tone wasn't loaded. He knew she just wanted to know.

"Nothing. At least not anything you're thinking."

She laughed and play-punched his arm. "Then tell me, stupid. What I like about you is your openness."

"Yeah. And you're going to think I'm crazy...or worse."

"Hardly. I know you well enough. Just tell me."

Mark moved to a sitting position in his bed. Lily followed suit. He drew in the sight of Lily's half-naked body. He could never get enough of her — her personality, her body, her warmth.

"I've got an ability, a strange one. Not a talent, and it's not natural. Supernatural, maybe. It's not a good thing. It's a curse.

"It started when I was young — real young. At the time, I didn't understand it at all and I assumed everyone could do it."

Lily mock-punched Mark again. "You have a habit of not getting to your point, dear. Out with it!"

He snickered. *She's right.* "Sorry. Old habits. From my first memories, I remember when I saw blood — maybe my mom cutting her finger, or a scrape on my knee — any person, including myself — I got strange feelings. It wasn't just seeing it either: feeling, tasting, or smelling blood could trigger it. It's hard to describe what I understood at that time — it was like someone was whispering to me, telling me the person who was bleeding was 'happy' or 'sad'. It was the closest concept I could understand at the time. Later, the whispers were more like thoughts, and they came from *within* me, not someone— somewhere—else. Its true source is still a mystery to me."

Mark noted Lily's serious expression. *She's listening to me. Seriously, she's listening.*

"What do you mean by 'happy' and 'sad'?" Lily asked.

"That's what it felt like when I was young — toddler young. It evolved, became more refined, and took a nasty, vile twist. It had nothing to do with the state of mind of the person whose blood I sensed, and I found—the hard way—what it really was. The whispers told me when someone was going to *die*." He stopped. He finally got it out. He waited to see how Lily reacted.

She didn't laugh. "You mean to the day, sort of thing?"

"No…yes. Sometimes. Geez, this is going to sound crazy now. I learned how it operated over many years — I had to sort it out through experience. If I see, touch or smell the fresh blood of someone — no matter how small a sample — the whispers rush in and tell me when the person will die. The further ahead in time, the less refined it is. If someone is going to die within the hour, I will know exactly when to the second. Beyond an hour, I will know it will happen within a day. Day within week, week within month, month within a year. I haven't sorted it out beyond that, but I know I can tell if someone is going to die within ten years. After that, it's just 'a long time'."

"Have you tested this ability — does it happen every time you make a prediction?" Lily was still starkly serious. Mark was so grateful, relieved.

"It's sort of the other way around. It's the fulfillment of my predictions that has helped me sort this out. The whispers are clear now, as clear as the timeframes allow. And it's never wrong for other people. I saw a spot of blood in a tissue of someone walking down the street—a complete stranger—and the whisper told me the person would be dead within the week. On a few occasions, I've foreseen death more immediately, and yet, I wasn't there when it actually happened. I saw a girl on a stretcher after a hit and run when I was twelve, and I knew she was going to die within the hour."

"What about you? You said you get the same 'whispers' when you bleed yourself but you mentioned they were never wrong for 'other people'?"

"That's the crazy, inconsistent part of the whole process," Mark admitted. "I know for a fact that what the whispers say about other people will not alter — it's preordained. But for me, it changes all the time. Most of the time, I'm told I'm going to 'live a long time', but sometimes, it changes. I've had a whisper that told me I would die within a year."

"Shit. When did you last read your blood?"

"A year ago. The whisper at that reading said, 'a long time', meaning when I'm old. But it oscillates all the time."

"I'm glad. I don't want to lose you."

"Are you sure? This is a crazy story. You could be moving in with a crazy man."

Lily kissed him. "I'm open-minded. I'd be lying if I said I totally believe you, but that doesn't mean I think you're crazy, and I certainly don't think you're lying. Stuff happens, and people interpret it through their own filters. That's the only way it can happen." She momentarily stared at her left hand, inquisitiveness etched on her face. "Do you want to read me?"

Mark shook his head with vigor. "No. Never. When you move in, I want to mute that shitty whispering. If I could, I'd kill it. That boy you saw in high school, the one who was serious and kept to himself, turned out that way because of the whispers."

"But, I saw through it, even then," Lily said.

"You're the only one that did. You need to understand one more thing about me. A lesser matter, but this cleans me out of anything you don't know about me. While the whispers often make me upset, there is a thrill I get from them, as well. Like having a secret power. Don't get me wrong — this is a curse, a horrible thing, but there's also something that gives me a charge from it."

"Maybe that's because it's part of you, whether it's good or bad."

"Yeah, that could be it."

Lily snuggled against him again. "I heard you say 'when you move in'. Is that an invitation?"

"Only if you can live with my curse."

"Of course."

***

Detective Superintendent Geoff Mitchell shouted, his face only a yard away from Mark's, "Are you telling me you can predict when people will die?"

"Yes."

"And this stupid blood thing. How does it relate to Lily?"

"When she moved in a few years back, I decided to do everything I could to avoid exposure to blood. People thought I had a phobia. I played to it. I knew Lily didn't *really* believe me — I was just grateful she loved me enough to accept me for who I am. That was enough for me. But early on, she wanted to test my ability and do a reading of her. I told her how I felt and she accepted it, begrudgingly. It was like that for a long time.

"Nine months ago, I heard her cry out in the kitchen — I raced over and saw blood on her hand. She cut her finger slicing sashimi. It flooded in; I couldn't help it. I'm just too fucking good at it. She was going to die within a year. More than a month, less than a year. It freaked me out, and Lily could tell. I broke down."

Mitchell paced the floor. "You're fucking crazy."

"Lily didn't think so. But I didn't tell her I knew she was going to die. I made the excuse that I fought off the prediction in my panic."

The detective slammed his hands against the table again, more red-faced than ever. "I can't believe this stupid shit! Is that why you killed her? You had to fulfill your own fucking prophecy?"

A small droplet of blood trickled out of Mitchell's left nostril.

Geoff's going to die in ten minutes.

Mitchell's eyes opened wide. "What's up? Your face has gone white. Am I close to the truth?"

Mark shook his head. "No, no, no." He pointed his free hand at the detective's face. "You're bleeding."

Mitchell wiped at his nose fiercely with his forearm. "More fucking crap!" He swung his fist with trained precision, with the impetus of rage, connecting with the side of Mark's face.

The detainee collapsed like a sack of potatoes to the floor, with the chair following him.

Denying the Thrill

***

When Mark tapped the hang-up symbol on his smartphone, he had a premonition.

He had told Lily he would be home soon and that he loved her. They said that to each other more often over the past few months, and it sat comfortably. Then he felt the smoldering coal in the deepest level of his stomach. *Oh God. It's today. Nine months in.*

It was the one thing he never revealed to her; the stark, unadulterated certitude that she was going to die within a year.

He walked quickly and tried his best to smile at the gallery's patrons without stopping to talk with them. On exiting the rear of the building into the busy nightlife of Little Collins Street, he jumped into his car and drove with zero consideration of the law or his safety.

I can't change fate. I can't change fate. And yet, he had to make the attempt. He had to try to save Lily's life.

He sped into Richmond in record time; attracting half a dozen blaring horn blasts from other drivers along the way. *Fuck them.* He screeched to a halt in front of the house, blocking a lane of traffic on his street. *Fuck them, too.*

Mark fumbled for his door keys and rushed into his townhouse.

There were several signs of a struggle. Upturned coffee table. Smashed vase.

Oh, God. Oh, God.

He stumbled around the several rooms that made up the lower floor of his home, hoping to find a sign — anything, of Lily. He entered their small kitchen and slipped on a large pool of blood, landing hard on the right side of his hip.

Oh, God. Oh, God.

He struggled to his feet and saw *something* on the floor, in the shadows of his pantry.

Something.

A scraping sound, coming from the small backyard, startled him.

Mark cried out, "Hey!" and briefly saw through his kitchen window a dark figure leaning against the glass — for a split second, he thought it was his own reflection. It was a male, but just a shadow puppet in the sparse light. The man's eyes glinted—the small reflection carried a thousand emotions: hatred, lust, unbridled hunger, and an evil as deep and dark as a coal pit. Just as quickly as he made an appearance, the stranger fled at a pace that defied human capability.

Mark was focused on the one thing that wrenched at his guts. *Lily*. He was close enough to see her clearly, despite the scant sources of light. He couldn't get too near, to hold her. She was entirely covered in blood; great splashes of it.

Lily will die in 5 seconds.

Her neck was a gaping maw, dripping with her dark red liquor. Lily's eyes were open, but unfocused. And yet, there was a single blink, followed by a gradual recession of her chest.

He stood on the wooden floor of his kitchen, his shoes sticky in her blood. Mark fell to his knees and screamed and cried in turn, and together, until all his senses collapsed into a singularity of despair.

For once, the aftermath, sensory rush did nothing for him, except more starkly outline his grief.

***

"You okay?"

The voice came from far away.

"Are you all right, Mr. Browning?"

The voice was clearer now.

Mark opened his eyes. The left side of his face hurt badly, and it was hard to get his vision in focus. He was in a tiny room, lying on a small bunk. A First Aid box was fixed to the wall opposite him. A face slid into view — a well-groomed man, suited up.

"Good. Just take it easy, mate. I'm Detective Inspector DeMeer. We found you unconscious in the interrogation room. We apologize for the attack on you...I hope you take into consideration Detective Superintendent Mitchell's state of mind at the time."

Mark tried to raise himself to a seated position but the policeman eased him back.

"How long have I been out? Where's Geoff?"

DeMeer frowned. "Only five minutes or so. We managed to open the room's door only seconds after you were struck. Our forensic team found shoe prints consistent with the perpetrator of the murder, and which don't match yours. We can also verify that the prints on the knife found in your kitchen aren't yours. We've just informed D.S. Mitchell that you are no longer a person of interest. He was upset — I'm sure you understand why."

A uniformed policeman rushed into the room. "D.I. Need to talk, Sir."

The detective left the room, indicating with a hand gesture for Mark to stay put.

A few minutes later, DeMeer returned, a frown now permanently etched on his forehead. *And a look of confusion.* "Mr. Browning. Detective Superintendent Mitchell collapsed and died a few minutes ago. It appears to be a heart attack."

Mark didn't bother feigning surprise. He touched the side of his face that had been punched and found it less painful than only minutes before. He licked his dry lips and felt a crack on the left hand side. He tasted blood.

You will live for a long time.

It always felt strange when his life expectancy changed. It just didn't make sense.

"Mr. Browning. I know this is hard, and you did have a good relationship with Geoff...Detective Superintendent Mitchell. Now that he has...passed — this is off the record of course — can you consider forgetting what happened to you? He was a gutted man...he had a long, distinguished career with Victoria Police. For his memory; for his family."

It took a full minute to register the D.I.'s request. He had, for the barest of moments, felt the thrill of his prediction of Geoff's death course through him. It always came a few minutes after the passing — stronger following an imminent death. "Huh? Oh, yeah. Of course. Under the circumstances."

DeMeer appeared relieved. "We're indebted, Mr. Browning. It's the right thing to do." He shook Mark's hand while closely inspecting his face. "I swear, I thought your cheekbone was fractured, but it's settling down very quickly, and looks all right. Do you want us to send for an ambulance to check on you, as a precaution?"

Mark managed the slightest of smiles. "I'm feeling fine. Just fine."

"You've been through a lot, Sir. I admire your resilience. It isn't easy to bounce back from a double tragedy."

"I just realized something. Learned something about myself."

"And what's that?"

"I'm *designed* to bounce back. It's the way I operate."

DeMeer was lost to him. The detective's face was expressionless but his eyes were curious...with a trace of fear and disgust.

Mark got to his feet and straightened his clothes. He shook DeMeer's hand again and left the police station.

He realized now that he could never deny the thrill.

A MOVEMENT IN THE SHADOWS
Edward Ahern

It was too big to be a rat's tail. *Possum tail maybe*, Fred thought. It lay in the overgrown grasses and weeds of his backyard, sprinkled with small, red ants trying to make a meal out of the hardened skin.

I need to chop all this down, he thought, looking around. *But why bother?* The backyard hadn't been used since his wife left with the kids nine years ago. The ropes to the tree-hung swing swayed listlessly, the wooden seat warped and mildewed.

He swung his arms to part the tall grasses, stepping carefully on the uneven ground. The yard was seventy-by-eighty feet, the view from outside blocked by heavily-matted shrubs and trash trees. When the kids were young, before his troubles, he'd kept it trimmed like a baseball field, but he hadn't walked back here in two years. With every step his feet sank into dead grass and leaves.

As he neared the stump of a maple tree, he noticed something yellow in the faded, brown ground cover, and kicked it. It flopped raggedly – another tail, maybe a cat. He felt a chill. *Good-sized predator's been using my backyard as a dining hall. Maybe set a trap? Don't have one.*

Fred retreated back into his house. As he moved through the kitchen and into his den, dust kitties scampered across the floors and into corners. His skinny frame thunked into his recliner and he tried to focus. *What the hell's prowling my yard? Never seen it, must hunt at night. Feral cat, maybe? But cats don't eat each other, do they? Need to ask around.*

15

He rummaged through a kitchen drawer, eventually finding an out-of-date telephone directory. "Hello, police? This is Fred Malone. I've got some kind of critter coming into my backyard and eating other animals – think I found the tails of a possum and a cat. How do I get rid of it?"

"Ah, sir, have you seen this animal?"

"No, no, but for sure it's dangerous, killing animals in my yard."

"Okay, and where do you live, sir?"

"828 Butte Valley Drive, here in Fairvale. Do you guys have traps I could borrow?"

"Just a second, please... We've had reports recently about missing pets in your neighborhood – two cats and a small dog. Have you found any animal bodies?"

"No, just tails. I saw a cat do that to a chipmunk once, laid it out and started chewing at the head, crunched its way down to the tail and just left the tail on the sidewalk..."

"Sir, will you be home tomorrow?"

"Yeah, I work from home, technical writer. Home most days, but I haven't seen anything in the..."

"Thank you sir, we should have the animal control officer at your house before noon tomorrow. Please just leave the remains where they lay, and don't try and capture the animal yourself. There's always a risk of you being bitten, and we do occasionally encounter a rabid animal."

"Don't worry, I'm not going back into my yard until your guy shows up." He hung up and winced. *Big, brave, ex-infantryman, afraid to go into his own yard.*

Fred worked on a product specification until 6 p.m., then shut down the computer and walked into the kitchen. He opened the freezer door and stared at three stacks of frozen dinners. *Chicken, beef or turkey? Turkey.*

After a microwaved dinner and two *NCIS* reruns, Fred went upstairs and got ready for bed. He was down to underwear and halfway between the sheets when he climbed back out and padded, barefoot, to the window facing the backyard. The moon was waning gibbous, with barely enough light to make out the lawn. He snorted. *Hasn't been a lawn in years.*

When he slid the window open, cool air fluttered against his undershorts. There was no noise or motion. Fred carried a chair over to the window and sat down, looking out into the still dark. He strained his eyes and ears, and after a few minutes, could hear the faint noises of cars cruising through the neighborhood, and see the blurred, dim lights from two of his neighbors' houses. But his yard was just a black pit.

Maybe install some motion-activated lights? Can't afford it. But anything could be down there and even with a full moon I wouldn't be able to see it. Maybe chop down the greenery? Take a chainsaw and a haymow, at this point. Maybe they'll bring traps.

***

The animal control officer arrived early the next afternoon in an SUV with a cage replacing the rear seat.

"Mr. Malone? I'm Officer Kudzma. Sorry I'm a little late. Let's take a look, shall we?"

Kudzma was short and wiry, with hard muscle cords. The two men tramped through the yard for fifteen minutes. Kudzma looked for scat, blood or animal remains, but found nothing. The ratty, yellow cat's tail wasn't lying near the maple stump anymore.

"Well, if there's something living here, it keeps a pretty tidy household."

Fred caught the implied doubt and ignored it. "Could you set a couple traps?"

"We don't do that. Too much chance that a pet, or, God forbid, a small child, gets caught in it. For sure, there's some animals missing from the neighborhood, but I don't see any problems here. Probably just some little varmint dining on roadkill."

Once Kudzma left, Fred took a forty-minute walk through his neighborhood. He hadn't noticed the weathered sheets of paper stapled to the utility poles: Gigi, a mustard-yellow cat, missing for two weeks, Oscar, a beige pug, missing for over a month. And a clean, dry sheet of stapled paper – Helmuth, a young, German shepherd, missing for two days.

Helmuth belonged to Gretchen Friedhoffer, a neighbor. On his way back to the house, he stopped and rang her doorbell. Gretchen opened the inside, wooden door, but kept the storm door closed as she talked to him.

"Oh. Hello Fred, have you seen Helmuth?"

"No, sorry." *Best not to mention my backyard tails.* "How did it happen?"

"Let him out two nights ago in the backyard, like always. It's a fenced yard, and he's never tried to get out before."

"Was there any noise? A car, maybe? If Helmuth was a pedigreed dog, maybe someone stole him?"

"I heard him bark a couple times, but he would do that any time someone walked their dog out front."

"Any blood or fur? Maybe someone shot him."

"No, no, no. Like I said, nothing."

"Okay Gretchen, I'll keep an eye out for him. He'll probably show up covered in brambles and smelling of skunk." Fred walked across the street toward his house. *Helmuth was young, but already forty, fifty pounds. Would take a big critter to bring him down without a loud fight.*

***

That evening, after defrosting and eating a chicken dinner and watching an old episode of *House*, Fred resumed his sentinel position at the rear window, this time, still dressed. He'd left the downstairs lights on in the back half of the house, but the electric lighting was no match for the outer darkness.

After twenty minutes of dark and quiet, he could hear the rustling of the grasses and shrubs in the drifting wind, and begin to see lighter and darker patches of black in the darkness. But leaving his mind and senses wide-open let old fears creep back in. *Just worry about what's taken over the yard.*

Then he heard a harsh cough and the sound of something dropping onto the dry, dead grass. He strained to see and hear more, but his senses were at their limits. A shrill crying began, mammalian shrieks of anger and fear, cut off suddenly by the thrashing of grasses, and then crunching noises for ten minutes.

I should go out and see what's happening...no better wait 'til morning. He sat in the dark room and stared out into his black yard for another half-hour, hearing and seeing nothing more.

The next morning, before coffee and breakfast, he grabbed a closed umbrella and went out into his yard. *Pretty pathetic self-defense. Nothing near the gate or walk to the back fence. God, this stuff is thick, nothing here, ouch, brambles. Wait, under the bramble bush, something has been digging.*

Fred poked with the umbrella tip until the scraped-over grass and dirt was pushed to the side. A short, hairy, gray-thing, perhaps three inches long, lay in the uncovered dirt. *Looks like a docked tail. Poodle maybe? But why bury it? Evidence, it's evidence.* He tore loose a handful of grass and used it to pick up the tail, the brambles tearing at his hand.

"Hello, police? This is Fred Malone again. I think a dog got killed and eaten in my backyard last night... No, no, I've got the tail. Looks like a poodle, I think.... You will? Okay, I'll wait."

The same motorized animal cage pulled up in front of the house two hours later. "Hello, Officer Kudzma. The tail I found is here on the front porch. I'll show you where I found it."

Kudzma took pictures of the tail, and of the little hole where Fred had found it. "Mr. Malone, we just got a report of a missing poodle. Minimillion. It was wearing a rhinestone collar with tags when it went missing. Did you find a collar?"

"No, sorry. Maybe you could set up one of those animal-safe traps?"

"Like I told you, we don't do traps. Have you, by any chance, been feeding any stray dogs?"

"I don't like animals, never have owned one. No way I'd feed one. Why are you asking? This isn't my fault!"

"Calm down, please. Never said it was. We just have to eliminate possibilities. What about your neighbors? Do they put out food for animals? Birds?"

"Not that I know of. I'm not really close to the neighbors, they kind of keep their distance."

"I seem to remember a blow-up you had, when you were teaching at the middle school?"

"That was a stressful thing, but it's ancient history now. I don't think any of my neighbors own a half-wild beast."

"It's peculiar, Mr. Malone. You sure you didn't see the dog coming into your yard? Taking a crap maybe?"

"No, officer, I didn't. I haven't paid attention to the backyard in years. Now, how are you going to get rid of it?"

"Not much to be done right now – no flattened grass where something has bedded down, no game trail in or out, no burrows that I can see." Kudzma hesitated. "Look, Mr. Malone, I remember the accusations and legal actions from ten years ago. If I start asking your neighbors if they saw an animal going in and out of your yard, they'll assume that it's yours, or somehow you're responsible. Best that we just both keep an eye out and see if anything develops. Chances are, you won't see or hear anything else, but in case you do, here's my card and cell phone number."

Fred took the card, not saying much more than thanks and goodbye. *I was never convicted, but I may as well have been. Wait and see? I don't think so.* Kudzma had triggered a memory, and he pulled his Chevy Lumina out of the garage and headed for a supermarket.

Once back home with his groceries, he pulverized a box of Ex-Lax tablets and kneaded the powder into four balls of high-fat hamburger meat. *Let's see how well you dine on these, critter.* He walked through the backyard, carefully lobbing the four balls into patches of thicker undergrowth. *Bet I hear some yowling tonight!*

Fred had bought one too many frozen, turkey dinners at the store, making the stacks uneven, so, he had another turkey dinner that evening; although he didn't really feel like turkey. He started to watch an episode of *Crime Scene Investigation*, but realized that he'd seen it, twice before.

He abandoned the rerun and took up watch from a chair at his bedroom window, camera in hand. After twenty minutes, he dozed, and woke up just before eleven. He put his head against the screen, but saw and heard nothing. *Just wasted ten dollars worth of meat and pills.* He held his post for another fifteen minutes, then stripped and went to bed.

He woke up when he felt a bug crawling down his cheek. There was something *wet* between his feet. He snapped on the light and cursed. There was a mound of feces and small bones on his sheet, the slime and liquid seeping out in a widening circle from the heap. *Jesus Christ! Jesus Christ! Jesus Christ!*

Fred pulled his legs up to his chin to avoid the offal, and rolled out of bed. *What the hell?* He stared wildly around the room. His bedroom door was closed, nothing seemed disturbed– *Wait, the window.* The window screen facing the backyard had been ripped, from top to bottom, in vertical swipes, and the screen edges were pushed back against the sides.

He stuck his head out of the window frame and looked down, but saw nothing, no movement. Fred ran back to the bed and pulled the top sheet off by the edges, then lifted the excretion off. He held the bundle at arm's length, carried it into the bathroom, and dropped it into the tub. As he turned, Fred caught sight of his face in the medicine chest mirror. There was a line of blood down his left cheek.

It wasn't a bug! He splashed water on his face, and then gently rubbed away the half-dried blood. A single, straight scratch ran from the top of his cheekbone to beside his mouth. *It could have ripped out my throat! But it didn't.* **Didn't?** *Maybe it's a warning? –Don't screw with me.*

Fred double-stepped downstairs and dialed 911.

"Fairvale police, what's your emergency?"

"An animal just broke through my window and crapped on my bed!"

The dispatcher broke into a laugh, and then caught himself. "Ah, sir, could you repeat that?"

After five minutes of back-and-forth, the dispatcher concluded that the problem wasn't a police emergency, admitted that the animal control officer (*There's just Kudzma,* Fred thought) worked only days, and assured Fred that the officer would be there as soon as possible, the next morning.

I'm on my own. He spent the next three hours nailing boards across his bedroom window, stripping his bed, and finding a bucket into which to throw the coagulated mess. Fred couldn't force himself to get back into his own bed, and slept for a few, fitful hours on the downstairs sofa.

Kudzma was at his front door a little before 8 a.m. "So, Mr. Malone, you believe an animal broke through your window, defecated on your bed, and left without a trace?"

"Look at my window! Look at the crap in my sheet! Look at my cheek!! You need to trap or kill this thing right now. Maybe analyze this crap for animal DNA."

"We're not capable of doing that. Um, your violent incident was unpleasant. Would one of your neighbors have done this? Maybe someone with a key?"

"Don't be ridiculous. The screen was pushed in from the outside. And nobody else has keys. Now that you're here, I want to go into the backyard for a closer look."

The two men walked around the house and through the gate. Nothing was visible in the grasses and weeds, but there were multiple, curved indentations on the back wall's cedar shakes, from seven feet above the ground up to the rear bedroom window.

"You see? It climbed up here. There's the claw marks."

"They're marks all right, but I couldn't say what made them. A woodpecker, maybe? A kid with a pellet gun? No animal I know could climb a vertical wall like this."

"You've got to do something!"

"All right, Mr. Malone, but there's only so much I can do. Tell you what, I'll set up two infrared motion detectors, like hunters use, and see if anything triggers the camera."

"You need to kill it."

"We don't know what, if anything, there is to kill. I'll set them up now and come back and check on them tomorrow. But, what I suspect, Mr. Malone, is that somebody who's upset about what you're alleged to have done, got into the house and did this. He could have cut and pulled in the screen, maybe even left the marks on the siding. You should change your locks." Kudzma turned to leave.

"What about the dead animals?"

"All we've got is a stub of a tail. Could've been planted. He's done his mischief, Mr. Malone, I don't think he'll be back."

I've got to protect myself tonight – the cops aren't going to. But what the hell is this thing?

***

Fred went online and plugged in a series of search words. After several dead ends, "Pet Killings Animal Monster", yielded an absurd, but frightening possibility. The website was flaky, but it reported animal attacks, since the 1930's, by creatures it called devil monkeys. The drawings were fanciful, the pictures clearly staged, and Fred almost closed the site to move on. Then he started reading the comments by frightened readers, all of whom reported nocturnal incidents like he'd experienced; pet killings caused by a large, monkey-like animal, with fanged incisors and sharp, three-clawed hands and feet, able to leap as much as twenty feet. *Nobody else will help me with whatever this thing is. Gotta do something.*

He pulled down the stairs to the attic, clambered up, and came back down holding an oilcloth-wrapped Remington 30-06 bolt-action rifle. He looked at the mounted scope pensively, then put the gun down and walked out to his car.

Moe's Gun World was a fifteen-minute drive. The store was as large as his supermarket. Fred walked back to the rifle section and found a salesman.

"I need an infrared scope for a Remington 770 Springfield bolt-action 30-06."

"There's a request I don't get every day. Let me look some things up." He returned with a boxed scope. "I've never used one of these, but the specs say it'll fit. If it doesn't, just bring it back. Have you got the right tools to mount it?"

Fred bought the scope, a wrench and screwdriver, and a box of ammunition, paying with a credit card that, luckily, wasn't yet over-extended. Once home, he removed the hunting scope and installed the infrared one. It was bulky, but didn't interfere with aiming or operating the rifle. He dry-fired the gun several times while aiming through the scope.

All right you ape, let's see how a copper-jacketed slug treats you.

He began pacing back and forth – kitchen through dining and living rooms and return – over and over, taking only a few minutes to microwave and eat a chicken dinner. *A single shot, maybe even two, shouldn't alarm the neighbors too much. They'll think backfire or firecracker. With a scope, maybe forty feet, how could I miss?*

Towards dusk, Fred pulled a board from the center of his bedroom window so he could aim downward into his derelict yard. He threw the board onto his mattress, the yellow, fecal stain churning his stomach. Bile rose toward his throat.

He forced himself to wait by the bed for a half-hour after sunset, and then stepped softly up to the window. He gently pushed the rifle barrel through the window opening and leaned against the nailed-in slats, sweeping the scope left, right, further away, closer in. *No napping this time, this time it's not some dog, this time you get to die.*

The minutes crept by ponderously, and Fred began shifting his weight from one foot to another, and changing his grip on the rifle stock. About a quarter-hour before eleven, Fred began to hear rustling in the tall grasses at the back of the yard. *Got a little burrow in and out do you? Show yourself.*

A shape lunged in jerks and starts, out of the hedges and into the yard. The picture through the night scope was so painfully sharp; he almost clinched his trigger finger and fired off a round. *Jesus Christ, what is that thing? It's dragging something, some kind of four-legged animal. Focus, asshole, what's it look like? – Stands on two legs, maybe five-and-a-half feet tall, hairy outline; black. Look at the teeth in that snout, could crunch an ox bone. Claws, definitely claws.*

Fred tensed, remembering his purpose, and leaned his eye into the scope. The muzzle flash, blast and recoil shook him out of concentration, and he forgot to work the bolt and chamber another round.

A hyena scream from the yard told him he'd hit it, but as he worked the bolt, the rifle was yanked out of his grip and tossed into the yard. Fred half-staggered backwards and, as he did so, something kicked in two of the slats in the window frame. Fred stood frozen by his bedside as a blue-black *something* swung into the room.

In the slow-time of panic, he watched it hop at him. *Not an ape, got no fingers, got claws, not hands and feet. Ape face though, canines big as boar tusks, biting, tearing, ripping...*

***

Officer Kudzma returned the next morning, at first light, a little after 5 a.m., *wincing* as he climbed out of the car, and walked directly to the backyard. He plugged the power cords back into the sensors, and then noticed where the rifle lay on beaten-down grass. "God damn it," he muttered. He picked up the rifle and jacked out the chambered round, then carried the rifle around to the front of the house and dropped it in the trunk of his car.

Kudzma jammed a pry bar into the doorsill, cracking it open. He walked directly upstairs and into the back bedroom. Fred lay on the floor, facing the ceiling. His throat had been torn out.

Kudzma sighed, then pulled out latex gloves, a plastic garbage bag and a large, folding knife. He severed the head from the neck, just below the bite marks, and slipped it into the plastic bag. The knife and gloves were tossed in and the bag cinched up. There was no longer any evidence of an animal attack.

After dropping the trash bag in his trunk, next to the rifle, he took out his cell phone.

"Frank...? Yeah, Kudzma... I think there's something wrong at the Malone house... Yeah, the guy with the animal complaint... Nah, nothing. I checked the two sensors I mounted last night and they didn't record a thing... Look, I'm gonna ring the front bell again, and if I don't get an answer, I'm gonna have to break in... Nah, no need to send another car. I got it."

He walked back into the house and stood in the living room for ten minutes, then called again. "Frank? Yeah, it's bad. Somebody cut off Malone's head and took it as a trophy...Yeah, I'll wait out front for them...Well, after what he did when he was a teacher, every parent in the neighborhood hated him...Yeah."

Kudzma stood patiently in front of the broken-in door. A surge of annoyance hit him. Once this place was sold and the yard cleared out, he thought, he'd have to relocate.

UPPING THE PRODUCTION VALUES
Ken MacGregor

Martin French had loved horror movies since he was six years old. His father took him to see, "The Creature from the Black Lagoon," in the theater; it had been his dad's favorite when he was a boy. As soon as the creature hit the screen for the first time, he was hooked. He asked his dad to get him all the classics: Frankenstein, Dracula, The Wolf Man, The Mummy. Martin's mother said he'd have nightmares, but he never did.

***

By the time Martin was fifteen, he was a horror movie expert. Plywood DVD shelves were bolted to the walls of his room, stocked with everything from, "The Abominable Dr. Phibes," to, "Zombieland."

When he was seventeen, Martin made a short horror film of his own: "Crushing Desire." It starred Martin's friend, Kelly, an eighteen-year old senior and fellow horror fan.

***

The film opens with Kelly wearing sweats and t-shirt. She is standing in a room that is empty, except for a large box. Kelly looks at the camera and smiles; she lets her sweatpants fall and puddle around her ankles. Kelly peels off her shirt; there's nothing under it. Looking into the camera again, Kelly pulls down her underwear. She runs her hands down her naked sides and tosses her hair back.

Kelly opens the lid to the box and climbs in. She somehow makes it seem sexual. She beckons to the camera, which moves in on her. Kelly closes the lid and squirms, touching herself all over.

She stops, eyes wide, as the box jolts. Kelly starts to panic as the box gets smaller and smaller, beating against the sides with her fists, until it slowly crushes her to death.

***

Martin built twenty-eight, identical and progressively smaller, wooden boxes. Kelly squeezed into each, until she could not fit in the last one.

The final shot was the outside of the smallest box; Kelly's voice-over screams faded to quiet as blood oozed out from the bottom of the box. Creepy music Martin composed on the computer added disturbing ambience. Martin edited it to look as if the box was shrinking on camera.

Martin entered, "Crushing Desire," in a Detroit horror film festival. It won the audience choice award. His dad grinned and clapped Martin on the back; his mom left the theater after her son's film and wouldn't meet his eyes until the next day.

***

On his eighteenth birthday, Martin only got one present.

"Oh-my-god! A Hi-Def Camera! No way! You guys rock!" He hugged both his parents with the hand that wasn't holding the new camera.

***

Martin and Kelly were sitting in the Chicken Shack. Martin was drinking coffee; Kelly had a chocolate shake that she was making last as long as possible.

"How would you like to be in another film?"

"Martin, you have a real gift, you know that?"

"For what?"

"Well, making movies, for one thing," Kelly said. "But also, you're kind of a born leader."

"I am?"

Martin didn't sound convinced.

"Last year, you convinced me to take my clothes off on camera," she tossed a mischievous grin at him. "I never thought I could do that, but you made it seem like nudity is the most natural thing in the world."

"That's because it is."

Kelly shook her head, smiling.

"Well, whatever this project is, you know I'm on board. I think you're brilliant, and I plan to ride your coattails to fame and fortune."

The waiter brought a thick, greasy cheeseburger, rare, on a plate with waffle fries and a pickle. He set it in front of Kelly, who thanked him.

"You eat that stuff?"

By way of answer, Kelly hefted the burger and took a huge bite. Thin, red juice dripped down her chin; she caught it with a napkin.

From his backpack, Martin pulled a sheaf of stapled pages.

"You wanna hear what it's about?"

Kelly nodded.

"Mm-hm." Her cheeks bulged with food around her smile. Martin handed her the script and she read while she ate.

Int. Dimly lit room, single chair in center, small window high on the cement wall. It is a basement, pipes running overhead. Water can be heard dripping slowly off-camera. MARILYN is in the chair, wearing a blue sundress. Her hands are tied behind her back, her feet bound to the chair legs; she is slumped over, unconscious. A FIGURE steps into frame wearing surgical scrubs. In the Figure's left hand is a straight razor, glinting in the meager light. Marilyn stirs, moans. The Figure shivers in anticipation.

Kelly swallowed hard and picked something out of her teeth. She didn't look up from the pages until she had read the whole thing.

"Oh, yeah. I am so doing this."

***

Martin had written Marilyn with Kelly in mind. A lot of directors use the same actors again and again. The male actor was new to them both; Martin knew him from film class, but hadn't worked with him before. Martin had written lines for the Figure, but James had a stutter; it was a bad one, and he couldn't do dialogue.

However, he looked great for the part; he was over six feet and broad-shouldered. He wasn't particularly muscular, but not fat either – just big. The lack of speaking lent the Figure an even more disturbing air; James's stutter was a blessing in disguise.

***

It was just the three of them and Martin's new camera in the basement. Also, the tripod, lights, light stands, boom and microphone. Martin was running all the tech himself; he set everything up before the cast even showed up.

Martin watched through the camera's small monitor as James lifted Kelly's head by the hair. The camera studied her face as the Figure did, and Martin thought she looked beautiful on screen, despite, or maybe because of, the bruise on her cheek and the burst capillaries in her eyes; makeup and contacts, but it looked very real – his makeup skills were improving, he thought, with no small amount of pride. Martin zoomed in as James leaned closer, his face almost touching Kelly's. He inhaled deeply, smelling her skin. Tentatively, he stuck out his tongue and tasted her cheek. Her eyes widened and flicked in his direction.

"Please," she whispered. "Please. I'll do anything. Just don't hurt me."

James put his finger to his lips and shook his head. He pulled the neck of her dress away from her skin with his free hand and used the razor to cleanly cut it from her body. The blade was real; it belonged to Martin's dad. He had a prop razor that looked just like it, on the table with the soda and snacks; later, they would use that for close-ups of skin cutting, adding the blood in post-production.

She held very still, watching the blade move inches from her skin. James sliced all the way down to the hem and through it; he peeled away the severed halves, exposing Kelly's bra and panties.

"Please," she said again. James ignored her this time and very carefully slid the blade under the bra at the join between the cups. The edge of the blade nicked Kelly's right breast, just a tiny bit, but it drew blood. James stopped; he, Kelly and Martin watched the trickle of blood as it ran down her ribs and abdomen.

That was not in the script. It was an accident, but it looked amazing on camera, so they kept rolling. Everyone was still in character, maybe more so than ever. James carefully turned the razor blade so it was facing away from Kelly and used it to slice the bra open. His free hand pulled away the separated cups, exposing her breasts. The blood was darkening the elastic on her panties, though it was slowing down and clotting already.

"I don't want to die," Kelly said, choked with fear and desperation. "Please, I don't care what you do to me, but please let me live. Don't hurt me. I can please you, I know I can. I can be a good girl. You don't need the razor. I'll cooperate, I swear."

James hooked her panties with a finger, pulling them away from her hip. He used the blade to slice the fabric, then repeated the procedure on the other side. He went behind her, grabbed her underwear by the back and pulled it off her, the camera catching the front of the panties disappearing between her legs. Naked, she began to cry. Martin tilted the camera up and zoomed in on her face; he even got an extreme close-up of one of her eyes as real tears fell. Beautiful.

"Cut," Martin said, quietly, stopping the camera and immediately turning off the hot lights. "Wow." James sat down as Martin unlocked the cuffs and untied Kelly's ankles. She got up and reached for a robe, but Martin stopped her.

"You'll smear the blood," he said. "Sorry, but you need to stay naked. Are you cold? I can get the space heater."

"No. I'm okay. I wasn't thinking."

"K-K-Kelly," James said. "I'm s-sorry I c-c-c-cut you." He gestured vaguely at her chest.

She smiled at him.

"Don't sweat it, James. It hardly hurt at all, and besides, it totally ups our production values."

"That's why I love this woman," Martin said. "She's a big-picture girl, all the way. I need to do the second set-up; James, will you help me move these lights? They should be cool enough by now. Just don't touch the bulbs: you'll get burned and they might explode. Seriously. Also, they cost a fortune. Thanks. Right over there. Good."

It took about fifteen minutes to get everything the way Martin wanted it and the actors in place; that was the beauty of a script where everything happens in a single chair. Martin checked the battery life and how much memory he had left on the chip. He was good for at least another hour.

***

The new camera angle was low, pointing up; Kelly's left thigh was in the foreground, out of focus. Beyond it, her still-bloody breasts and face were visible. Martin had added more bruising on her arms and torso, mostly finger marks. He had also added several new cuts to her shoulders, abdomen and legs, though these were simulated with fake blood. Kelly was, once again, bound to the chair. She and James were waiting; Martin just stared at them for several seconds, mind racing. He looked at his storyboards and then at the tableau in front of him.

"Ready?" Martin asked.

"I'm s-s-sorry, Martin," James said. "I s-suddenly have to p-p-p-pee."

"Shit," Martin said. "Go upstairs. Make it fast."

"No," Kelly said. "Don't, James. Stay here. Piss on me."

Nobody moved or said a word, for several seconds. James looked at Martin. He looked back at Kelly.

"W-What?"

"It fits the scene." Kelly's jaw was set.

"If you want Marilyn to be peed on, we can work that in, but I can fake it, Kelly," Martin said. "I think I have some Gatorade in the fridge, upstairs."

"Just hit *record*, Martin," she said. "It will look better on camera if it's real. It's what the Figure would do, and you know it. James, you go ahead and do it. Martin and I want this film to be as good as it can be, don't we, Martin? Go ahead, James; I don't mind, really."

"This is fucked up, Kelly," Martin said.

"I'll d-d-do it," James said. "But you c-c-can't t-tell anyone." Kelly smiled at him.

"It'll be our secret, James," Kelly said.

James looked down at himself. Martin hit *record*. James pulled down his fly and reached into his pants. Kelly's eyes got wide as James pulled it out. Martin watched in the monitor, as James pissed on the girl tied to the chair. He started on her thighs and arced it up her belly and breasts; then he pissed on her face. She whipped her head back and forth, trying to escape what was happening to her. It was sick and fucked up and looked amazing on camera.

After, James went to the utility sink and washed his hands. Martin kept the camera on Kelly. Her head slumped. Urine dripped from her hair. The razor was on the chair next to her. The water was still running, off-camera.

Kelly wriggled in the chair, pulling at the ropes holding her wrists. She got a hand free, just as the water stopped. She snatched the razor and quickly put her hand behind her back.

James stepped into frame. Martin's heart was pounding behind the camera. He was still rolling. There were twenty-seven minutes left on the battery.

James, as the Figure, leaned over her. He flicked his tongue out, like a snake.

Kelly's hand whipped forward. The open blade flew across James's throat. Blood arced out and James jerked back.

He fell on his ass on the stone floor, holding his neck with both hands. His eyes were huge.

"K-K-K-K-"

His eyes glazed over. Blood soaked his shirt. Kelly looked at the dripping razor in her hand and back to the big man on the floor.

Behind the camera, Martin swallowed hard.

"Cut."

James fell back, limp. Kelly looked at Martin. Her eyes shone in the work lights.

"I already did."

"Jesus. What have we done?"

Kelly untied herself from the chair. She set his father's straight razor on it and pushed her hair back. Stepping close to Martin, she smiled. He could smell copper and piss.

"We made a movie, babe. A *real* horror movie, just like you wanted. And you know what? I can't wait to do it again."

Martin turned off the camera and the hot lights. He stared at James's body on the floor. The blood had stopped, but there was a lot of it. Kelly called his name from by the stairs.

"Can I use your shower? I'm a mess."

RABBIT MAN
Joseph Rubas

(Editor's note: Originally appeared in the January 1979 issue of Amazing! *magazine* by Timothy Warner*).*

Situated roughly half-way between Washington, D.C. and Richmond, former capital of the Confederacy, Fauquier County, Virginia, is today known primarily for its lush, rolling horse pastures and quaint antebellum era architecture. Like many rural areas, however, Fauquier hides more than a few dark secrets.

Established on May 1, 1759 from land once belonging to neighboring Prince Williams County and named for Virginia's then Lieutenant Governor, Francis Fauquier, Fauquier County remained obscure until the Civil War, when several small skirmishes (mostly power struggles over the nearby Orange and Alexandra Railroad) broke out. General Lee and his Army of Northern Virginia passed an uneventful several days in Bealeton in 1862, Lee remarking: *"This,* this beautiful, unspoiled land...*this* is why I fight."

After the war, Fauquier's population grew slowly but steadily. In 1900, Virginia's governor at the time, William "Billy Boss" Akins was involved in one of Virginia's earliest car crashes near Warrenton, Fauquier's seat, and succumbed to his wounds several weeks later. Local tradition holds that if you stand on the spot where the crash happened (today a little traveled farm road), you can hear the sounds of smashing metal and breaking glass (at night, naturally).

In 1942, several local boys were killed in the Pacific Theater of World War II, one of them, John Farmer, being posthumously awarded the Medal of Honor for bravery in battle. Shipped in by train, the bodies were held in state at Warrenton town hall for several days. Stories of their restless spirits haunting the marble halls of city governance abound.

In the early half of the present decade, with evidence of wrongdoing from both the White House and the military becoming common knowledge, trust in government plummeted. Scattered reports centered around the military complex at Mount Warrenton (ostensibly a communications facility) began making the news. In September 1974, a group of motorists traversing US 17, near Opal, claimed to have seen a strange, unidentified flying object moving ponderously in the night sky, a "giant blimp-shape" trimmed with twinkling, running lights. Still others claim to have been harassed by soldiers when coming too close to the base. A young man who wished to remain anonymous told the *Washington Star* in 1976 that while he and his girlfriend were driving along an unpaved road through the hills, they were surrounded by men in vehicles and told to turn around or be shot. Investigative reporter for the *Richmond Democrat,* Steven Faye, attempted to question Brigadier General Allister Holliday, head of the Warrenton facility, in 1977, but the general had no comment.

As juicy as these legends may be, however, the strangest (and most well documented) involve neither ghosts nor extraterrestrials.

It began on a hot July evening in 1970. 18-year-old Richard Johnson and his 16-year-old girlfriend, Peggy Stevens, were parked at an isolated area known locally as Kelly's Ford. "It's a very rural place," says local historian Benjamin Haskins, "there's an old, disused railroad trestle over the river and lots of forest. Kids have been going there to hang out since the twenties."

While sitting in Richard's four-door Dodge Station Wagon and talking, the lovers were confronted by a strange and terrifying sight.

"We were talking," Richard said in a 1978 interview, "and all of a sudden, this...this *thing* comes out of the woods to our right."

The "thing" appeared, in the headlights, to be a six foot tall rabbit, replete with ears and a cottony tail.

"He was carrying an ax."

Richard says the "rabbit" lunged for the front end of the car, slamming his ax onto the hood and yelling, "You're trespassing and I have your number!"

Understandably frightened, Richard threw the car into reverse and drove away, the rabbit man in hot pursuit.

"He tried to catch us, but when he realized he couldn't, he threw the ax." The ax smashed through the car's back window, before careening away into the dirt.

Local police scoured the area, but could produce no evidence. The nearest town to Kelly's Ford was well over ten miles away, and no property near the spot was held privately. Without leads, they concluded that it was simply a prank.

"Kelly's Ford is a notorious lovers' lane," Fauquier Sheriff Jim Bradly said in *The Washington Post,* "someone was probably sick of all the kids going out there and tried to scare 'em."

The story was popular in Virginia and D.C. for a time, but fizzled out.

Then came the second attack.

On October 28, 1970, a retired construction foreman named David Myers was walking along a dirt road south of Kelly's Ford. It was near midnight and Myers, who suffers from insomnia, was ambling along the moonlit lane when a strange sound stopped him in his tracks. "It sounded like someone chopping down a tree."

Curious, Myers continued on. A hundred feet from the spot where he first heard the noise, the road bends left into a stand of trees. On the left-hand side of the road, an abandoned house sits (even today) in virtual ruins, last inhabited by an elderly lady who died in 1953. Local children claim it is haunted.

"When I got to the house, I saw a giant rabbit on the front porch, chopping at one of the porch columns with an ax."

The "giant rabbit" noticed Myers, and flew into a rage.

"He said, 'All you people trespass around here!'"

With that, the rabbit man lunged at Myers, who managed to outrun him.

Concerned now, the police launched an intensive manhunt, focusing on the Kelly's Ford section. On December 1, 1970, they found something.

A body.

"She was partially buried along the riverbank," Sheriff Bradly said. "Most of her was covered with leaves. It looked like some animals got ahold of her."

The woman was twenty-five-year-old, Sandra Conner, who was reported missing on August 18, 1968. An autopsy revealed that she had been killed by several blows to the head, most likely from an ax.

"That's when we really knew we were dealing with something serious."

The story received national attention. MAN IN BUNNY SUIT SOUGHT IN MURDER read a typical headline from the *Daytona News-Journal*, dated December 15, 1970.

Says Bradly, "This sort of thing was new to Fauquier. People were scared. And we really didn't know how to handle it."

The Fauquier County Sheriff's Department was inundated with calls from people claiming to have seen the Rabbit Man. Many were false alarms. Some were more ominous.

"A 12-year-old boy said the Rabbit Man chased him when he tried to cut through the woods on his way home from school," Bradly said. "When we looked into it, we found an ax and a chipmunk nailed to a tree."

On January 27, 1971, 75-year-old Mavina Melvin, a leader in the local black community, was found slain in her home ten miles from Kelly's Ford. A hatchet still jutted from her chest.

Reports of Rabbit Man activity skyrocketed. By the spring of 1971, a special task force had been set up at the behest of Virginia's Attorney General.

Still, the horror continued.

Rabbit Man

On March 5, a man out fishing near Kelly's Ford was attacked in broad daylight. He was saved by a passing motorist, who said a large man in a dirty rabbit costume fled into the woods.

Three weeks later, a night-watchman at a Culpeper grocery store, just over the Fauquier line, was found hacked to death in the parking lot of a McDonald's.

On April 21, a woman was attacked when she got into her car to go to the store. It was past midnight, and, she claims, when she looked into the rearview mirror, she saw the Rabbit Man sitting in the back seat.

"Get out of my car!" he raged, and she was only too happy to oblige.

Reports began to taper off, and by the autumn, the Rabbit Man hadn't been seen in nearly six months.

Following the hysteria of 1970-'71, the Rabbit Man made only sporadic appearances. In April 1972, a man walking down a back road in Bealeton claimed he was shoved down from behind by the Rabbit Man. "You smell like booze, so you lose," the Rabbit Man supposedly said.

In November 1973, a gas station attendant in Goldvein was assaulted by a man in a rabbit costume who came out of the woods. He survived but lost vision in one eye.

Following the Goldvein attack, the Rabbit Man went on hiatus. As the search ramped up (and the story became national news), confirmed sightings stopped. Nearly two years after the last assault, in September 1975, a nine-year-old boy was found blood-caked and screaming along a rural stretch of road by a passing trucker. He lapsed into catatonia before he could relate his tale, but regained consciousness in early October and told police that he had been abducted from a Culpepper shopping center by a man driving a black Chevy van; accosted from behind, he didn't see his attacker's face.

Knocked unconscious during the kidnapping, the boy woke hours later in what he called a "campsite" in the woods. He was chained to the bumper of the van, and the man, now sporting a dirt-crusted rabbit costume, was standing over him with a club.

The boy was intermittently beaten for nearly twelve hours before slipping his confines while his captor slept.

Police immediately sprang into action. The macabre "camp" was found on October 11 along a tributary south of Kelly's Ford. Consisting of a crudely built cabin (the roof of which was covered with blue tarp) and a decaying shed, the camp yielded more mystery than it solved: Bone fragments, bearing signs of being pulverized with a sledge hammer, were found scattered through the surrounding forest, as were several other items, including a black-and-white snapshot of a woman tacked to a tree. The woman was eventually revealed to be Wanda Jenkins, a Washington businesswoman who graduated from Fauquier County High School in 1957. The photo was ripped from the 1956 copy of Fauquier High's yearbook, and the name below her picture had been scribbled out. Police spoke with Jenkins, now married to a beltway insider, but she was unable to assist.

The last confirmed Rabbit Man incident occurred on June 28, 1976. A family who wishes to remain anonymous claims the Rabbit Man spent several weeks spying on them and wandering through the woods behind their house. The first to see him was the family's 11-year-old daughter; her testimony was quickly dismissed. Strange happenings persisted, however, and, eventually, the matriarch glimpsed the Rabbit Man moving through the bushes late in the evening.

On June 28, the Rabbit Man broke in through an unlocked window and confronted the daughter with an ax, calling her "Whore, liar, Democrat," before being chased away by the father and older brother.

During the chase, the father tackled the Rabbit Man and pulled off his mask; no one caught a glimpse of his face, but they had his mask.

"That was two years ago," Sheriff Bradly says, "and we still have nothing to go on."

While evidence is lacking, supposition is not. A popular rumor circulating in Fauquier County, circa 1974, was that the Rabbit Man was a local mechanic who noticeably suffered from schizophrenia. Neighbors claimed he trespassed on their properties late at night and tried to look in their windows. Another suspect was a Vietnam veteran who suffered shellshock in the war. He, too, was known to prowl his neighborhood. While the schizophrenic mechanic could never be found (and was considered a fictitious character), the Vietnam vet, a twenty-nine-year-old named David Amplas, was proven to have been in a state mental institution during the crimes.

On September 14, 1978, an unsigned letter appeared in the *Richmond Democrat* claiming that the Rabbit Man was a severely mentally ill "young man" who was being "controlled" by his mother and his psychiatrist...the writer of the letter. Popular lore has it that the Rabbit Man is actually the spirit of a mentally retarded youth who was killed by a group of bullies near Kelly's Ford in the 1940s.

Yet another popular legend holds that the Rabbit Man was an escaped mental patient named Robert Yaras who was confined in 1958 after killing several prostitutes in Virginia and the Carolinas. Yaras disappeared from the Staunton Hospital for the Criminally Insane in 1960. He spent several years of his youth in Fauquier County, and would thus be familiar with it. Yaras, however, was discovered in Canada in 1983, and had been there since at least 1968.

A prison guard in Tennessee claims that one of the inmates under his charge admitted to being the Rabbit Man in 1977. Further investigation turned up no such inmate, and under questioning, the guard admitted to inventing the story, "To get famous."

Another prison guard, this one from Texas, says that one of *his* inmates is the Rabbit Man. His story is more creative, for what it's worth. He claims: The Rabbit Man is actually "Leatherface" from the popular movie *The Texas Chainsaw Massacre*, which chronicles the brutal murder of four teens at the hands of a cannibalistic family in the backwoods of Texas. He goes on to say that "Leatherface" escaped capture and wound up in Virginia, trading his mask made of human flesh for a rabbit costume. When authorities in Texas located him, they kidnapped him and took him back under the cover of night, much like the Israeli's did to Nazi Adolf Eichmann in 1960. [ED: Eichmann was captured by Mossad in Argentina on May 11, 1960, and executed in Israel on June 1, 1962. The operation to take him down was secret and caused an international incident.] His story has several holes, however, the most damaging being that the events of *The Texas Chainsaw Massacre* supposedly occurred in 1973, three years after the bulk of the Rabbit Man attacks. Additionally, *Chainsaw* director, Tobe Hooper, when contacted for questioning, confirmed that the movie was fiction, and that such a "massacre" had never happened, despite its claims of being based on a true story. (It was based on the crimes of Wisconsin cannibal Ed Gein, who shot two women in the mid-fifties and decorated his home with the proceeds of various grave-robbing expeditions).

As it stands now, the Rabbit Man is still at large, though his crime spree seems to be over. Police are still seeking evidence and the people of Fauquier County are still uneasy at night. Who knows? Maybe the Rabbit Man is still out there even now, waiting to strike one more time.

GRASSHOPPER
Ellen Denton

When I was in my junior year of high school, the factory my father worked at burned to the ground, leaving its four hundred employees scrambling to find work. Jobs in a small town are hard to come by, but we all did our part.

I learned from the school guidance counselor that one of the teachers, a Miss Anna Linus, mentioned wanting to find someone to help part time with household chores. She lived with her sister, Emily, in a large, Victorian home, inherited from their parents.

I went to Miss Linus's classroom to recommend myself for the job, and assured her that, if hired, I would work diligently at whatever was needed. She was a rosy, rotund woman, with an ear-to-ear smile and laughter in her eyes. She cheerfully hired me on the spot.

I was to work for three hours each day, after school; six hours on Saturdays, and was to start the next day.

***

The three-story Victorian was on the outskirts of town on two acres of well-maintained, landscaped grounds. The house was quite imposing looking from the outside. To the right of it was a neat row of painted sheds, the largest greenhouse I'd ever seen was off to the right, and a fine-looking tack and stable house, made from tumbled stone, was to the left, now devoid of horses.

If the well-manicured grounds and stately structures hadn't looked as regal as they did, I wouldn't have been so surprised when the front door was opened to my knock by the broomstick-thin, sour-faced sister, Emily, and revealed what I can only describe as a vortex of filth and decay within.

On that first day, when I walked into the wide entryway, there were black, plastic bags, filled with foul-smelling trash, piled up against the walls, waiting for monthly transport to the town dump. When I timidly ventured to ask why they didn't place the garbage outdoors in cans, and then have the cans emptied weekly by the sanitation department (as was the normal custom in town), Emily Linus looked at me with annoyance and pointed out, as though it were obvious, that the big, metal trash cans would besmirch the appearance of the grounds.

I was next shown into what appeared to be a formal drawing room that, under other circumstance, with its high, ornamental ceilings and breathtaking stained-glass windows, would have been magnificent.

Now, however, the corners of its floors, walls, and ceilings were festooned with cobwebs thick as bird's nests. The threadbare carpet was stained everywhere. There was a large, decorative wood table with a busted leg that lay on its side, with stacks of old magazines and newspapers spilled from it onto the floor in a yellowed, haphazard heap (which I later learned had been there like that for the last two years). I could also see, peaking out from under a ruffle of floral upholstery at the bottom of a chair, a mousetrap with a dead rat in it, now mostly gristle and bone.

***

I was then given a tour, by the expressionless Emily Linus, through a few other rooms in the house that were on that first floor, and soon saw that most of the surfaces were coated with inches of accumulated dust, some of it dotted with dead flies.

I had to restrain myself from gagging when I entered the kitchen because of the smell from rotting food left in the stack of unwashed dishes piled up on every counter. There were dead cockroaches floating around in a cauldron of oily water sitting on the filthy stove. I almost slipped, at one point, on a chunk of greasy meat on the kitchen floor.

After seeing a few more spaces of similar ilk, I reminded myself how badly my family needed money and how scarce jobs were, forced an eager look onto my face, swallowed hard, and turned to Miss Linus.

"What would you like me to do first?"

I was relieved when she told me to check the flower beds encircling the house, for weeds, adding the comment that, "You can never put too much time or work into keeping the outward appearance of a home looking lovely." She then explained that her sister, Anna, would be returning late from the school that day, and that she would be the one to assign me further tasks when she arrived.

***

You could have practically gotten down on your hands and knees with a magnifying glass to find any weeds in the beautiful and well-tended beds, which I soon learned Emily saw to personally, along with the lavish plantings in the greenhouse. The rest of the grounds were cared for by a full time gardener.

Anna Linus didn't show up that day while I was there, but she did on the day after that, which was a Saturday.

That's when I got to see the second floor of the house and heard something *alive* moving around on the third.

***

The second floor was every bit as horrible as the first, and in some cases worse — with one exception.

Emily Linus's bedroom was as fresh, sculptured, and beautiful as the grounds surrounding the house. There was not a speck of dust anywhere. The four-poster bed, the slipcovered chairs, and the long, billowing curtains were cheerful looking and spotless. A lovely cherry-wood writing desk sat in one corner and hook rugs brightened the floor. The entire room smelled like springtime, which I soon saw was because of a large vase of lilacs on a bedside table and a bouquet of yellow roses atop a bureau. I was not actually shown this room by anyone, but took a peak inside when I knew the two sisters were occupied with something downstairs and would not catch me snooping.

That day, I'd been brought to the second floor by Anna, who wanted me to remove all the boxes and trash in a library so that she could get at the books. There was a lot to do, and it would take me at least the entire six hours of that first Saturday.

The work was extremely unpleasant because of the rodent droppings and cobwebs. On top of that, the library smelled so terrible that I began habitually checking my watch to see how much longer I would need to be there before my six hours were up, and I was relieved when I finally had only an hour left to go.

I was walking down the hallway with one of the remaining boxes to place it in an unused bathtub, when I heard a dull thump on the ceiling above me.

I stopped and looked up for a few moments, and then heard it again, except this time, it was five thumps in rapid succession, and there was urgency to the sound, like someone knocking on a door, desperately needing to get in or out right away. There was a pause of about thirty seconds, and then three more thumps, this time slow and deliberate. This was followed by a prolonged wail, muffled by the layers of floor and ceiling above me. The pained sound rose in pitch, until it became an unearthly scream, also distant and muffled but sharp enough to make the hair on my arms stand up.

Sure there was someone alive up there, I raced downstairs to the two sisters, who were sitting in the drawing room, and asked them about it.

They both stared at me in silence, with identical, emotionless expressions – which is when I realized for the first time that the laughter constantly visible in Anna's eyes was actually the gleam of insanity.

It was she who finally spoke. "It's nothing dear, just rats or water in the pipes. This is an old house. Go back to work."

Her usual, merry smile, which had only faltered for a moment, returned to her face, and Emily Linus now looked as stiff as a totem pole.

I did as I was told, but there was something unsettling about what had just occurred. The more I thought about the sounds and the sisters' reactions when they knew I'd heard them, the more I felt there was something wrong going on – more wrong than just two eccentric women living in a filthy, decaying house.

***

I worked Monday through Friday of the following week, on both the first and second floors, but never heard those sounds again. I couldn't get them out of my mind though, and never felt convinced by Anna's explanation of what it was. There was something too insistent, focused, and human about those thumps – and the *wail*.

I decided that the next time I was working on the second floor and knew the sisters were busy elsewhere, I would sneak up to the third and look around quickly, just to dispel my concerns.

That day came on Saturday. There was a storage room at one end of the second floor that Anna wanted me to rearrange, which would take me several hours.

After working awhile, I ascertained both sisters were still on the first floor by going downstairs and asking if it was okay to get a drink of water from the kitchen (which I did, from my cupped hands, as I was afraid the smudged, foggy-looking glasses might be diseased). They were both occupied – Emily worked from home as a bookkeeper and was in her office doing just that, and Anna was in the drawing room polishing her toenails and humming to herself.

When I got back up to the second floor, I made some noise by pushing around boxes in the storage room so that the sisters would assume I had gotten back to work.

I pulled my shoes off and tiptoed back down the hallway to the curving, marble stairway leading up to the third floor.

I had, mid-week, casually asked Emily what was up there, and she'd told me it was just some additional bedrooms, devoid of any furniture, and an office, also now empty, that her late father had used. I remembered that conversation well because of the way she kept staring at me after she answered the question.

I got to the top of the stairs, and in under a minute, had checked the doors on the third floor. Unlike the ones in every room below, every door up here was locked.

I was very disturbed by this. The situation reminded me of some B-grade, horror movie; where a person is being held prisoner in the attic or basement of a house by some crazy person. I kept telling myself there was nothing like that going on here, and I was just letting my imagination run away with me.

Then I would look at some revolting corner of this crypt-like, Victorian monstrosity, (which seemed to get darker and dirtier every day), or look at Emily's lined, stark face or Anna's strangely gleaming eyes, and I could again easily believe there was some terrible thing going on up on that third floor. I also, through seeing Anna on almost a daily basis, realized the bright smile she always wore was rigidly fixed onto her face as though glued there. It was even present when I once ventured into a sitting room and found her napping in a chair, her teeth still gleaming brightly from over-stretched lips. If I reported my suspicions though, and it turned out that it was nothing but some rats in an empty room, it would cause needless embarrassment for the sisters and would surely cost me my job.

I needed to find a way to get into the locked, upstairs rooms.

***

On Wednesday of the following week, Anna assigned me some tasks to do on the second floor and informed me that she had a headache so would be lying down in her bedroom for awhile, and that if I needed something, Emily would be working in her office on the first floor. It was now or never.

Again, removing my shoes, I padded up to the third floor and went to the room I thought the sounds had come from when I'd first heard them above me the previous week.

I pressed my ear up against the door, and then knocked gently. No sound came from the room. I decided I was being ridiculous and started to turn away, when I heard a scraping inside, then a feral snarl that crescendoed into the unmistakable scream of a human voice.

I once used my laminated library card to spring the lock on our basement door when I couldn't find the key, and that's what I was going to attempt with this one.

I wedged it into the space by the doorknob and worked it back and forth and up and down, turning the knob this way and that, until I heard a *click*.

I grabbed the doorknob and then jumped nearly two feet into the air when I heard Emily Linus yell, "STOP!" from the other end of the hallway.

I turned to see her racing toward me with a horrified expression on her face. When she reached the door, she shoved me away so hard that I tripped and fell. She then pulled a key ring from her pocket and relocked the door with shaking hands.

When she turned to me again, she looked devastated.

"I'm so sorry. I didn't mean for you to fall like that, but you have no idea what..."

She turned to look at the door, and then back at me again. Her almost impossibly white face was a mask of desperation and anguish. By now, I'd gotten over my initial shock and stood back up.

"There's someone in there! I know for sure there is now. I heard them. You're keeping someone imprisoned in there!"

"No! I swear to you, it's not what you think. There's nobody in there right now."

"Then why is it locked? Open the door and let me see!"

She looked resigned, and as though every last bit of energy suddenly drained out of her, she bowed her head and slid down to a sitting position against the wall to the side of the door.

"The only thing I'm afraid of is what will happen to you, if you do go in there. I told you my father had an office up here, but that wasn't true; it was a laboratory and it took up much of this floor. But, I wasn't lying when I said it's empty. Right now, at this very moment, I swear to you that there is absolutely nothing in there. When there is, you can hear it, just like you did a little while ago."

***

We sat at a table in the breakfast room, which, like the rest of the house, was festooned with spider webs and wet, wilting boxes of junk and slime-encrusted pieces of this and that. There were ruffled floral curtains on the window that I could visualize having once been bright and cheerful, but which were now so encrusted with dirt, I had to avert my eyes from them to not feel ill.

Emily Linus poured us both a cup of tea. A few minutes before, I'd watched her use a piece of steel wool to vigorously scrub the insides of the cups, but that still didn't eradicate the black, stained-in dirt around the rims. When she placed the tea in front of me on the table, I put my hands around the cup in a show of polite gratefulness, but couldn't bring myself to put my mouth on it.

Emily saw this and smiled sadly.

"Would you believe, just five short years ago, this entire house was as pure and beautiful as the grounds surrounding it?"

"Like your bedroom?" The question slipped out before my mind could get a hold of my tongue.

She looked at me sharply, and then nodded with the same forlorn smile. "I guess I do owe you an explanation about..." She looked around and made a sweeping gesture with her arm. "About all of this. I never meant for anyone to come here. Hiring someone was Anna's idea."

She stared down at the table quietly for a while, then, with a resigned sigh, looked up at me.

"My father was a scientist and a brilliant man – quite visionary, actually. He had some theories, though, about things considered *far-fetched* – things like the existence of other dimensions and parallel worlds, to the point that, he soon became an object of ridicule and scorn in the scientific community.

"He became so rabidly unrelenting and fanatical in his demands that time and money be invested into researching these areas, by the government facility he worked for, that he eventually lost his job. Whispers that he was a madman got around, and doors everywhere slammed in his face when applying for further work.

"He had a sum of money stashed away and used it to turn most of the third floor into a private lab where he could pursue his research. He became a recluse once he did."

Emily grew silent here, and I saw a true smile flicker across her face for the first time since I'd met her.

"He was an unparalleled genius. During the ensuing years, he created things never before seen in heaven or on Earth.

"He came running out of his lab one day holding an object that looked like nothing more than an ordinary fountain pen. He called Anna and myself into the parlor to watch as he clicked this pen-like object while aiming it at a vase. The vase elevated three feet into the air. Within a week, he was able to make this table we're sitting at now – and the four chairs surrounding it – rise up to the ceiling and hover there for a full minute, before slowly descending back to the floor.

"Another time he created this little box with wires and lights all over it that would make things disappear when placed inside it – first, small, inanimate things like stones or coins – then, living creatures he kept in his lab, like mice and frogs.

"So, you see, he truly was quite gifted and brilliant, perhaps more so than anyone else in this world.

"But then, he began working on something that he said would vindicate him in the scientific community. He never said what it was, but he became obsessed and often would not leave the lab for days, even sleeping there.

"One day, there was a sound like the winds of hell, and every window, wall, and floor of the house – and every object contained within – shook so hard, I thought the end of the world was upon us. Things crashed to the floor; even the light bulbs burst in their sockets. This went on for three horrifying minutes. Both Anna and I feared there'd been an explosion in the lab, so we ran up there and called out to my father and banged on the door.

"There was no response. We were never allowed to enter the lab without his permission, but of course, in this case, I pulled out my keys, and fearing the worst, opened the door.

"And it was to a completely empty room.

"Every single thing – every object, every counter, stool and tool, every living creature from my father himself to the mice, rats, rabbits, and snakes he kept there for his experiments, every notebook and scrap of paper – it was all gone. Not so much as a curl of dust remained in that room."

Emily now pushed back from the table and stood up. "You don't believe me!"

She was right. I already had my doubts when she started talking about her father's improbable inventions, but when she told me about the complete vanishment of the lab, I was sure she was making it all up in some desperate effort to keep me from telling anyone about the person imprisoned up there. She read these thoughts on my face.

"I guess I have no choice but to let you see for yourself. We need to hurry though, before Anna wakes up from her nap."

The last thing I wanted to do was go up to some makeshift prison with someone I was now convinced was completely insane and probably dangerous. I needed to think fast. I looked at her apologetically.

"It's just that it's such a fantastic tale. Please continue. I promise to listen with a more open mind."

"You'll listen with an open mind when you see for yourself that there is no one in that room."

She took me back up to the third floor, warning me that, no matter what, I must not step one foot into the room.

With one hand, she grabbed my arm with the force of a vice to prevent me from doing just that, while unlocking and opening the door with the other. She then – standing behind me and grasping me by the shoulders – positioned me so that I could clearly see that the room was completely empty. She then just as quickly closed and locked the door again.

"But the sounds I heard – there was a human voice."

Emily Linus looked toward the stairs at the end of the hall, and then spoke in a whisper.

"Things disappear from that room, but sometimes they come back – just not in the same condition in which they left."

What she told me next was so fantastic, that if she hadn't showed me one final thing as proof before I left that day, I would not have believed any of what she said, and would have just assumed that the entire story was only the delusional rantings of a deranged mind.

***

She led me back downstairs and out onto the beautiful grounds, and then over to the greenhouse. Before she began speaking again, she placed her hand against the outside of the structure, as though the life and beauty of the flowers and plants within breathed life into her through the glass.

"A week after the lab vanished, our pet dog, a Regal-looking bloodhound, went into the room and he, too, disappeared without a trace. I kept the door closed after that, until a week later, I heard his familiar bark coming from the room.

"Overjoyed at his return, I ran up there and threw open the door.

"It was him; I knew that unquestionably because he wore the bejeweled collar I'd once gifted him with, but he had three heads now, and the arms of a monkey sprouted from his back.

"This mutated monstrosity bolted towards me, so I slammed the door shut a moment before it leaped out of the room. For the next hour, as I sat outside the door weeping, I could hear all three dog heads howling and whining like a chorus of the damned in hell. Then it stopped, and when I dared to crack the door again, the creature was gone.

"A month later, our father returned. Anna was closest when we heard his muffled voice coming from behind the locked door, so she unlocked it and ran into the room before I could stop her. I heard her scream just as I reached the door and saw a rat-headed, snake-tailed monstrosity speaking in the human voice of our father, while it writhed on the floor in reptilian slime, coiling around Anna's legs. Then both of them vanished into thin air.

"She returned days later, and through the door, assured me that she was okay, and she was – at least on the surface. When I cracked the door, I could see her body was not changed in any way, so I let her out of the room, only to discover that whoever it was that returned – was not Anna. Some cursed creature – walking death, or demon – now crouched in the portly folds of Anna's flesh, and proceeded to take over her life. I never opened that door again, no matter what I heard moving or speaking within."

She concluded this bizarre tale by telling me about the house itself.

"Bit-by-bit, this home turned into what you see today. It began to slowly die, day-by-day, room-by-room, becoming filled with the darkness, dirt, and putridity that had taken over Anna. She would touch something and it would darken or fade. Ever since her return, some force from that room seemed to flow through her hands and press down onto the house.

"For some reason though, she had no power or control over the grounds, or anything beyond them. Her suffocating influence was confined to the house by whatever forces had her in their grasp. Outside of that, such as at her teaching job, she carried on the charade of being a normal person.

"Over time, I came to realize, for reasons I know not, that flowers and plants dulled the fires of her destruction, at least outdoors and within my own room, which is the only place in the house I can counter-balance what she does. I grow them in the greenhouse, to ensure I have flowers to place there year round.

"Come with me back to the house now. I'm going to pay you for the week you just worked. You shouldn't ever come back here; it's not safe."

As we returned to the Victorian, still stately and impressivelooking from the outside, I realized the only thing I knew for sure was true, because I did see it with my own eyes, was that no one was locked in the room on the third floor. Everything else she told me, however, was simply too incredible to be believed. I felt sad for this woman, who I now assumed was harmless, but completely insane. Until I remembered one thing she said that nagged at me with a hook of truth.

It was about the inside of the house slowly dying. Even in the short time I'd worked there, it did appear to get darker and more hideous every time I looked at something newly. The once cheerful curtains in the breakfast room were filthy the first time I saw them, but when I looked at them again that very day, while in that room with Emily, I saw they'd become so weighted down with additional dirt and grease in the few short days since seeing them last, that the curtain rod sagged in the middle. Spider's webs that festooned the corners of a bedroom on the first floor had, in less than a week, grown and spread by many feet, now dangling like sheets of lace from the ceiling, far faster than any spiders could possibly have spun them.

Once back in the house, Emily started counting out money to give me from a pretty madras purse. She looked pale and sad.

I thought of something that would tell me if there were at least some crumbs of truth to any of her story, or if she truly was, along with the always, strangely-smiling Anna, insane.

"Miss Linus, why didn't you ever leave this place? Why don't you leave it now?"

She looked at me for a long time, and I could tell she was struggling with something within her own mind, and debating with herself whether or not to tell me something. She then looked resolute and turned away. "I can't leave. That's all."

I walked over to her and gently placed a hand on her shoulder. "Tell me."

She turned back to me, starker and sadder than I had ever seen a human being look.

"I told you that things disappear from that room, but sometimes come back, just not the way they left. I didn't know that at first, so, I once walked into that room, too.

"Some of the things my father kept in the lab, before it vanished, were tankfulls of bugs that he used for his experiments. He favored grasshoppers. Green grasshoppers."

Emily Linus always wore loose, long-sleeved, high-necked dresses, that came down below her knees. She stepped back to put some distance between us, and starting at the neck, began unbuttoning the one she was wearing now, until the entire front of her body was exposed. As soon as I saw her hinged, green torso and six spindly legs folded tightly across it, I knew that every word she had told me that day was true.

***

When Emily Linus closed the front door behind me that day – when I left that house for the last time – I knew then that I would never return there. In fact, I avoided even passing by it for the remaining four years I lived in that town, before I married and moved away.

Today, I returned to visit old friends, after being gone for almost ten years. The three story Victorian was gone. I heard it had one day simply collapsed like an imploding star – rotted timbers and termites were the general consensus in town. No one knew what happened to the two sisters who had lived there. Their bodies were never found in the debris. The two acres of property, and the structures that still remained standing, fell to some distant cousin.

When I went by there, whatever was left of the fallen house had already been carted away, and there was a "for sale" sign up.

I walked across the grounds, which had been long untended and were now in a state of wild, weedy dilapidation. The greenhouse was still there, and I could see the blackened, wilted remains of the plants and flowers that had once flourished within. There were cracks radiating out across the glass on all sides of it, but outside, on one wall, a scraggly, thorny vine scrambled up to its roof. It bore a single, lovely yellow rose. A grasshopper clung to it as it waved a little in the breeze.

THE MANY DEATHS OF PRIVATE STANHOPE
Adam Millard

Reginald Whittaker glanced around the small, cold office. A large, ornate bookcase filled the opposite wall, and the desk at which he sat took up the rest of the room. Hanging upon the walls were several framed photographs of a man Reginald recognised. There was a full platoon shot, in which the man from the photographs and Reginald sat, side-by-side, staring towards the camera with expressions of anticipation and fear. 1914, that photo had been taken; Reginald had contained a youthfulness about him; an innocence that the years to follow would wipe away completely. Reginald averted his gaze from the picture before the inevitable tears had a chance to seep from the corners of his eyes.

Just then, the door opened. The elderly gentleman, who had welcomed Reginald at the door fifteen minutes earlier, shambled through it. He looked, to Reginald, close to death; his liveried skin suggested an ailment other than simply old age, and his gait was that of someone struggling to maintain balance. He also had the countenance of an aristocrat, which was not beyond the realm of possibility, since Reginald had made a point of inspecting the house and its gardens before committing to an audience with the fine fellow.

"Sorry to keep you waiting, Mr. Whittaker," the genteel man said, as he closed the door behind him. "I'm currently up to my neck in taxes, and the paperwork is something of a rotter."

Reginald nodded. His neck cracked, reminding him that he, too, was almost in his twilight years. "Not to worry," he said.

"I've already cancelled the domino-match in which I was to partake. Have you heard of the Swan with Two Nicks?"

The man shook his head in dissent. "I'm not a drinker, Mr. Whittaker." He smiled, more out of courtesy than anything else. "Let's just say that the tipple and I are not, nor have we ever been, very good friends."

The thought that this man, this immaculately-dressed and distingué gent, had, at some juncture in his life, battled with the demon, Booze, was incomprehensible, but such was the way with aristocracy. Reginald had neither the money nor the idiocy to become an alcoholic; though things might have been different if he'd been offered the chance back in the twenties, when it had been easy to be led into a debauched existence by any number of miscreants masquerading as friends and colleagues.

"I received your letter last week, as were your intentions," Reginald said. He couldn't, for the life of him, fathom the meaning of the correspondence, and if he wasn't intrigued, to say the least, he might have been a little less predisposed to attend without suitable knowledge of what he was actually turning up *for*. "I've noticed the photographs peppered around the room. Would it be presumptuous to assume that I am here regarding a certain, Walter Stanhope?"

The man's lip curled up; what should have been a smile was actually more of a sneer. "You would be correct to assume such a thing," the man said. "I believe that Walter and yourself were stationed together during the First World War." It wasn't a question; the man knew exactly of their connection.

"For three years, yes," Reginald said. "We used to call him The Cat, for reasons you are probably not familiar with."

This seemed to strike a chord with the man, for he smiled genuinely, something that Reginald had not seen since making the gentleman's acquaintance that afternoon. "Oh, please, I'd love to hear how he came about such a wonderful moniker." His eyes creased, a hundred crow's feet spread across and into the fellow's diminishing hairline.

Well, Reginald thought. *Why not?* The domino-game was already postponed, and he had very little else to be getting on with.

He requested a glass of water before starting, and the old man said he could do much better than that, producing a bottle of fine scotch. When Reginald offered the man a cursory glance, he simply smiled and said, "Just because one doesn't imbibe doesn't mean it's not on hand."

So, with a glass of warm, golden heaven in his hand and a lit pipe in the other – the smoke from which the elderly gent had no reservations about – Reginald began.

"The first time it happened was 1916," he said, sipping ponderously from the glass. "Messines Ridge, a *hell* of a place to be in the winter, I'll tell you..."

***

As they rushed for the small, German pillbox, bullets whizzed through the air. One of them clipped Tommy Russell's ear, but he didn't stop running. That would have been stupid. Reginald didn't think they were going to make it; the pillbox was a lot further away than he'd previously believed it to be, and he wouldn't have suggested making a break for it, if he had known the true distance.

The gunfire was coming from *everywhere*. It was a wonder they were all still standing. The only possible explanation, Reginald thought, as he leapt across a ruined trench, was the riflemen's indecisiveness over whom to shoot first. There were five of them, and surely – should the shooters settle upon just one of them – it would decrease their numbers more successfully. Instead, they were haphazardly spraying fire over the area, hoping for some good fortune.

The men reached the pillbox – which was hexagonal in construct, and barely camouflaged – and threw themselves inside. Surprisingly, Reginald was the last in; even Tommy Russell, with his blood-drenched ear, made it before he did. He made a mental note to work on his fitness-levels, should the chance ever present itself again.

"Is everyone okay?" Reginald asked. To Tommy he said, "How's that, Private?" He extended a tremulous finger towards Tommy's sopping earlobe.

"Just a graze," Tommy said, patting the side of his head gingerly and wincing as the pain hit him. "Could have been a lot worse."

"Did anyone see the shooters?" Wally Stanhope asked. He was doubled over in an effort to catch his breath.

"I didn't know there *were* any until after we started running," Private James Croft, exclaimed. "If I had, do you think I would have done it?"

"That's exactly why I didn't tell you," Reginald said. "We all *made* it, didn't we? Most of us in one piece." He signalled to Tommy's ear.

"The trouble is," Private Sidney Walker – *Sid* – said, "we're now stuck in the middle of nowhere with lord knows how many riflemen waiting for us to stick our heads out. Not the best idea in the world, Reg."

"They've been onto us for miles," Reg reminded them. "If we hadn't found this place, we'd be out in the open and dead by the end of the night." He paused, surveyed the pillbox, then added, "No, they won't come anywhere near us, not tonight, anyway. Too scared of getting shot, themselves."

After around an hour of back and forth, trying to concoct a plan of action that would get them back on the safe side of the ridge, Wally Stanhope stood, hoisted his rifle up onto his shoulder, and said, "We can't just wait here for them to figure out a way in." The other four soldiers exchanged confused glances, unsure of what Wally considered as an alternative.

"General Plumer knows where we are," Reginald said, hoping that he wasn't lying. "Give it a few more hours and the cavalry will come rolling in. There's—"

"Not a chance in hell that Plumer's going to risk the rest of the platoon to pull our sorry behinds out of here," Wally interjected. Whatever he had planned, there was no talking him out of it.

"So, what? You're just going to walk out there and hope the riflemen are having a tea-break?" James asked. "It's *suicide*, Wally."

Walter Stanhope was not a stupid man; Reginald actually thought him the most intelligent in the platoon, which was exactly why what he was suggesting made no sense at all. "He's right, Wally. We don't even know where they're positioned, or how many of them there are."

And then, for reasons unbeknownst to the rest of them, Private Walter Stanhope smiled. "Well, I guess we're going to find out."

For ten minutes, they tried to talk him out of it, but he was insistent. They were to watch for the gunfire through the front loopholes and attempt to take out the source; Wally would simply do his best to dodge any incoming fire. It was a ridiculous plan. In fact, it wasn't a plan at all.

It was *preposterous*.

Wally told the group to make sure they fired true, for his life depended on it, and Reginald told him that there was no way, not in a month of Sundays, that any of the survivors would feel an ounce of responsibility or guilt if he was taken out by the enemy.

"I wouldn't expect you to," Wally said, and then he was on the outside of the pillbox, running for the adjacent woods. Snow filled the atmosphere, fluttering in each and every direction, like miniature butterflies. And then, the first shot came, whipping up a white miasma, as it pounded into a drift. At the front of the pillbox, Tommy, James and Sid returned fire. Tommy began to shout aloud that he had managed to get one of the bastards right in the face, though whether that was true, they would never know. At the rear of the fortification, Reginald said a quick prayer for Wally, for he didn't expect the man to return after such an ill-conceived gesture that was bordering on stupidity of the highest order.

The Many Deaths of Private Stanhope

***

"So, what happened?" the man asked, leaning across the desk to fill Reginald's glass. "We both know he didn't die."

Reginald sipped whiskey, savoured the burn, first on his lips, then at the back of his throat. "We couldn't *believe* it, when he returned almost an hour later," he said, eyes wide open as if to demonstrate just how shocking it was. "He was covered with snow from helmet to boot. He looked like the abominable snowman, whatever one of those looks like. At first, we all thought he'd been shot. There were red patches in the snow, especially around his mouth. We got him cleaned up as best as we could; Tommy asked him how he managed to avoid being shot. Do you know what his reply was?"

The gentleman chortled. "I couldn't even hazard a guess, Mr. Whittaker."

"He told us that it was easy to evade enemy-fire once you'd decapitated the enemy." Reginald shuddered as if a goose had wandered across his grave. "At the time, we just laughed. Tommy said Wally was cuckoo, in a manner of speaking, but we didn't mention it again. As far as I was concerned, it was just good to still be among the realm of the living. I managed to keep a few things to myself, too; things that would have unhinged the rest of the men."

"Go on."

"Wally's coat, once we'd wiped the snow away, was covered in bullet-holes. He took me to one side and told me they were glancing shots, but there was no way so many bullets could come so close and yet, miss." Reginald began loading tobacco into his pipe. He hadn't noticed until now, but his hands were shaking, as if the momentary nostalgia had put the fear of God into him. Tobacco was scattered nervously along the desk's edge, and Reginald found himself apologizing before brushing the minuscule, brown dregs into the palm of his hand and dropping them back into his gilt-trimmed tin. He relaxed back in his chair; the leather creaked beneath him. "The next time it happened, it was just me and Wally. We'd been in a trench on the outskirts of Arras for almost two weeks. The Canadians had secured Vimy Ridge, and when the news reached us, we managed to get hold of some wine with our last pennies, and we intended to celebrate and toast fallen comrades, as was the way it was done, back then. Would you believe we even managed to acquire a bottle of Crème De Menthe? Anyway, news had come, from Field Marshall Haig, that the chances of attaining some prime positions were good. As you can imagine, although it was frowned upon, we all embarked on a jolly good knees-up..."

***

"Tastes awful," Reginald said, handing the bottle across to Wally, before spitting against the trench wall. "Where did they get this from, again?"

Wally took a hearty slug from the bottle, wiped his lips with the back of his hand and said, "Squiffy McNee's lot raided a bombed barracks over in Nantes. Apparently, there were cases of the stuff." He drank some more; the sound of distant bombs dropping did nothing to perturb him.

There were cases of the stuff, Reginald thought, *because nobody was crazy enough to drink it.* His mouth felt violated, and he'd only taken a sip. He walked across to the corner, picked up the Crème De Menthe, which would at least take the edge off the wine's astringent aftertaste, and proceeded to glug thirstily from it.

They had much to celebrate that was for sure. The Canadians had done well to take Vimy, and Reginald's platoon had a clear run at some key targets. But tonight? Tonight was for drinking. The rest of the men were camped further along the trench; the sound of merriment was audible above the explosions from over yonder. Wally had suggested keeping the first bottle to themselves, before joining up with the rest of the platoon; Reginald, who had tasted the state of the putrescence in the bottle, would gladly forfeit his share of the booze.

An hour later, and Reginald was still relatively sober – insomuch as any infantryman who had not imbibed so heavily for almost two years. He had a nice, gentle buzz, the kind of mystical thrum that was both warm and welcome. Wally, on the other hand, was pissed as a newt, slurring his words to the extent that Reginald had taken to simply nodding as a retort.

It was raining heavily outside – and, to a certain degree inside – but it was met with a level of felicity. The snow from the winter had taken its toll on the men, with several dying from exposure and more as a result of the subsequent afflictions. The rain had its own drawbacks, of course, but at least it didn't make the terrain impossible to traverse, the way the blizzards had.

Reginald wouldn't have even noticed the rain, had it not been for Wally's removal of the trench tarpaulin. He had been blissfully in a world of his own, the effects of the alcohol bringing dancing stars to his vision, when all of a sudden, he found himself getting wet very quickly.

"Jesus, Wally! What are you playing at?" Reginald pushed himself away from the edge of the trench to better his view. Wally was already scaling the side of the gorge, kicking mud and dirt down onto his scattered webbing and personal effects. Somewhere, off in the distance, another bomb exploded, its rumble almost knocking Wally off-balance. "Where the hell do you think you're going?"

But it was no use; Wally had drunk enough of the nasty stuff to knock his senses for six. He staggered up, further and further, finally managing to drag himself completely out of the trench.

"Wally, you're going to get yourself killed, you fool!" Reginald called up to him, but he paid no heed. There was a good chance he hadn't even heard Reginald's reproach or the concern tainting his tone.

He turned in to face the trench, and to Reginald, he looked tiny way up there above the berm. He was grinning, though his eyes were shut tight. In the darkness, Reginald could have sworn he winked the moment before he fell inwards.

Reginald made a sound deep in his throat, the kind of noise that can only emerge when something terrible is happening. He wanted to catch the fool, to race across and break his fall, but there was no way he could cover the distance in time. Instead, all he could do was watch as Wally fell through the air, almost in slow motion.

And then, when he made contact with the ground, caving in his bugwarm in the process, there was an audible crack as loud as the bombs falling off in the distance. Wally's head was pointing away in an unnatural direction; the top of his spine pushed out against the flesh at the nape of his neck, the way a pen might stretch parchment.

Dead, Reginald thought. The barmy idiot had only gone and broken his own neck.

Dropping to his knees, with the fine, yet terrible rain, peppering his exposed neck and hair, Reginald planted his face deep into the palms of his hands and began to sob. This was not how it was meant to go; tonight was in celebration, and now Reginald had a lot of explaining to do. Corporal Simmons was a fair man, but even that wouldn't save Reginald from this mess. If he wasn't shot for this, he would, at the very least, be tossed in a chokey.

But Reginald needn't have been worrying himself with such silliness. The prone and twisted form of Private Walter Stanhope was *moving*, contorting itself back into a more acceptable shape. It was the sound of cracking – like chicken wishbones being snapped – that made Reginald lower his hands. He was just in time to see the bone from Wally's neck sink back into its proper position.

For a moment, Reginald was speechless. He sat there, paralyzed, apart from his mouth, which flapped open and shut like a fish out of water. Wally seemed to be composing himself, too. He brushed the mud and grime nonchalantly from his knees and elbows, before straightening his posture.

"H. . . *How?*" Reginald finally managed.

But Wally was in no mood to explain. He simply skittered backward along the trench and slumped in the far corner. Over the distant bombing, Reginald could hear the words...

***

"'I'm not drunk any longer'."
The man had listened to the tale raptly. He was perched upon the edge of his leather chair, his hands knitted together so tight that his knuckles were white. Eventually, he shrugged. "That's quite a story, Mr. Whittaker," he said. "Could it be that your eyes deceived you? That Walter was, in fact, unharmed by the fall? I'm no doctor – though I *could* have been, had I taken more interest in my studies – but something as serious as a broken neck would be impossible to recover from, especially the way in which you described it."

"I know!" Reginald said, almost spat. "And there were more instances just like this. I watched him fall at the Battle of Verdun, only to reappear without a scratch, three days later. He'd somehow managed to drag himself along a road, into some trees, where he'd kept a low profile for almost forty-eight hours, before daring to attempt a return to base. Some old comrades of mine swore blind, pardon the pun, he'd taken a bullet to the eye during Passchendaele. That was when we gave him his nickname. *The Cat.* Private Walter Stanhope had nine lives, that was for sure, and yet, there was nothing any of us could do to prove just how odd it was."

The genteel man stood from his chair for the first time. He wandered across to the photographs adorning the wall and gazed, silently, at them for what seemed to be forever. Eventually, he turned; a small grin played upon his lips, and his left eyebrow was raised. "What if I were to tell you that you were, indeed, correct?" he said.

"Excuse me?" Reginald said, all of a sudden feeling more than uncomfortable in his surroundings. There was a palpable eeriness about the atmosphere, now. The fine hairs on the back of

Reginald's arms perked up and danced around, as if the room had become statically charged.

"All those times you believed Walter dead," the man said, returning to the desk. "What if I told you that you were right?"

This, Reginald thought, must be some kind of terrible set-up; and if it was, there was something deeply deplorable about the whole thing.

Reginald stood, and immediately felt better. The man in front of him was of no threat. *Sure*, they were both elderly, but the man was more advanced in years than he, and Reginald thought he would be able to get by him without too much trouble, should the need arise.

"I have to leave now," Reginald said. "This has clearly been an error on your part. I thank you for the hospitality, but unfortunately..."

It was at this point that the man reached down for the doorknob and twisted it. Reginald believed it to be for his departure. He was shocked, and once again paralyzed, as if inflicted by a mild stroke, to discover a man standing between the doorframe.

A man that couldn't possibly be, and yet, *was*.

"Wally?" Reginald gasped, clutching his chest, as pain wracked through him. His legs threatened to give way beneath him, and all the time, the man – the esteemed gent with whom Reginald had rather taken a liking to, but not anymore – was smiling.

The man between the doorframe *was* Private Stanhope, and yet, there was something missing. He was older, but not as old as he *should* have been, and his eyes were deep and dark, like chasms looking into the very depths of hell. His face was haggard, loose, as if it could be torn away from the skull beneath with the merest of effort.

"I...I don't understand..." Reginald said, almost choking on the fetid stench, which accompanied Walter Stanhope.

"It really is quite simple," the man, who Reginald had spent the best part of an afternoon, recounting stories to, said. "Walter

Stanhope, here, has been dead for longer than you could possibly imagine. He was dead *before* he enlisted, back in 1914. Before my own mother fell pregnant with me, in 1890." Behind him, Walter was snarling, drooling black spittle down the creases of his flapping jowls. "You see, Mr. Whittaker, there are things in this world that neither you nor I can comprehend. If I should tell you that Walter Stanhope maintained his youth by feeding upon the flesh of German soldiers, would you believe me? Or perhaps, that he would tear the throats from enemy officers, in an effort to remain youthful and, therefore, keep this secret from you, what *then*?"

Reginald shook his head, never once taking his eyes from the aberration standing opposite. "This is impossible! Lies, all *lies*! What has he done to you, Wally?"

The man took a step back, allowing the beastly newcomer entrance to the office. "I fear we shan't be seeing each other again," the man said, slipping out through the door and into the dimly lit hallway. "But, I want you to know that it is nothing personal; merely a request, on behalf of my associate."

He pulled the door shut as he exited, leaving Reginald and Wally alone in the office. By the time the screaming ceased, the man had made a pot of tea and scattered cucumber sandwiches upon a silver platter. He returned to the office to discover Walter had made something of a mess.

"Was it really necessary?" the man asked the beast, which was becoming younger by the second, thanks to the fleshy repast. "It will take forever to clean this lot up."

"Oh, don't be so persnickety, Charles," Walter said. He looked like his old self again, after almost six months of inexorably ageing. *The power of the flesh*, Charles liked to call it.

"It's not as if you have anything *else* to be going along with, is it?"

Walter was right, although Charles wasn't to be outdone. "And who, pray tell, will be contacting the next one? I do believe I still have my uses."

Walter had sidled up to the photograph hanging upon the wall. He began to run his spindly finger along the line-up of soldiers. When he was satisfied, he tapped the glass. "This old boy should do," he said, his jagged teeth still covered in meaty morsels.

"As you wish," Charles said, settling down to his desk. As he wrote, he couldn't help thinking that the cucumber in those sandwiches would repeat on him something terrible that evening. *Oh, well.* Ultimately, it was worth the pain, which was Walter's theory, too. He didn't *enjoy* feasting upon veterans, men that he had pleasurably fought alongside, but they were the only things that sustained him. And he was running out of options.

"*The Cat?*" Walter snorted, picking Reginald's head up from the office floor and staring into its wide eyes. "How very *droll.*"

"Indeed, Walter," Charles said, his pen darting across the paper before him. He sighed, drank his tea, and finished writing the letter.

Dear Sidney Walker,

I hope this missive finds you well and that the years have been kind to you. You don't know who I am, but I wish to meet with you to discuss something of utmost importance. My address is Bintree Manor, The Street, Dereham, Norfolk, NR20 5NE. It is with great anticipation I await your response.

Sincerely Yours,

Charles Beauregard

WENDIGO'S WOODS
D.M. Kayahara

We never heard it coming. We had been on the canoe trip for three days and never knew anything was following us. Maybe it wasn't, maybe it just stumbled upon us.

***

The sun is just starting to set and we have the fire going. The sky is still bright enough for me to see it as it bounds into our campsite. It is a mess of matted fur and mud or dried blood, I don't know. It smells like death and moves like a man pretending to be an ape; or an ape pretending to be a dog. It covers ground quickly, sometimes on all fours, sometimes on two legs; whatever helps move it fastest past the canoe, the woodpile, our tents.

I can't understand it – and can't say anything – but I must be making a face because Trent looks behind him. I'm not able to warn him in time. When he turns, the thing slashes at him. I don't see how; Trent still has his back turned to me but suddenly there is too much blood. Across from me, Jen is screaming and Mark is babbling something over and over again. I'm not sure what Roger is dong beside me because he's quiet and I'm frozen. Trent turns back toward us. His hands are at his neck but they can't hide the mangled wreckage of his throat. Sinew and tendon flex and slip as Trent's hands try to keep his head from falling loose. His hands drop, his head rolls back and we are staring at a lifeless stump where his face had been.

It all takes just a second. I don't know how a thing like that can happen so fast but it does, and just as fast, I'm up and running. I look back twice. The first time, I see Mark trying to hit it with the small hatchet we'd brought to split wood for kindling. I think about how he'd told us we needed to pack light and how we wouldn't want to carry more than we'd have to. I get a flash of a terrible thought: somehow, in my panic, I think he's probably regretting not bringing the bigger axe. I am frantic and I am horrible. I hate myself but I don't stop running.

The second time I look back, the thing is kneeling on Mark, bringing the hatchet down again and again, until there is nothing left but spray and the sound of metal hitting dirt. The thing is covered in the blood and bones of my friends. It howls with something that sounds like glee. It looks like a monster playing at being a man. I do not see Jen or Roger and I don't stop running.

***

I'm being clawed at by branches and brambles as I go. Some piece of wood or stone catches my foot and I go sprawling at a speed too fast for me to recover from. My right shoulder hits first, losing a battle to stay whole, against the trunk of a tree. My arm is suddenly behind me and doesn't seem willing to come back. I know it's still there because of how badly it hurts. My left knee hits second, as I come off the tree, and I feel my skin split. I'm up as fast as I can manage, staggering more than anything, and trying to keep my gasps as quiet as I can. The wind's gone out of me and I can't get it back.

***

That's when I see the cave. The sunlight is almost gone, but I'm moving slowly enough to see it. It seems as good a place to hide as any. I half wonder if I'm walking willingly into the lair of the beast, but I have no other options. I can't outrun it now and I need to hide until I have a shot at it. I climb the slope to the entrance, bump my shoulder on the way in and struggle to get as far inside as I can before the stars that cloud my vision fade into a darkness that overtakes me.

***

When I come to, I can't tell where the smell of smoke is coming from, and I can't see anything. Our camp should have been too far away, and it smells like things that are not meant to be burnt. It smells like rot and rubber, like shit and skin. For a second, I think that maybe the smoke will mask my smell and I should try and run, but I don't know if it even hunts by smell. I stay still. I wait for my eyes to adjust to the darkness, but they never do. There is no moon. No light outside the cave. I remember my phone falling in the river within the first few hours of our trip, when Trent flipped the canoe. I had been angry then. I am sick to my stomach with frustration now, but maybe it's just the smell.

I try to feel the ground around me, to find a wall and get my bearings. Nothing within reach of my left arm. My right arm is still a lightning storm attached by an ill-fitting joint. I kick out with my feet, still find nothing, and try to push myself along the floor of the cave on my side, in search of anything at all. I'm slow, afraid I'll hit my shoulder again, afraid I'll lose more time or be caught, unconscious, and never wake again. I don't know if I'm getting closer to, or further away from the way out.

When the glow reaches me, I realize that I made it much deeper into the cave than I had first thought. The mouth of the cave was hidden by a bend and the fire I was smelling is close enough to be casting light on walls and getting brighter. I am able to see well enough to make it to a wall and back to my shaky feet. Smoke is creeping into the cave and I realize I have no choice but to leave, before I'm suffocated or caught by the flames. I stumble to the bend in the cave, stoop low, and try to peer around the corner without being seen.

***

The fire is directly outside the mouth of the cave. It has been built with some wood but is also fuelled by tent poles and backpacks and coolers. It's everything we had and it is all burning. It takes a second for my eyes to adjust, before I see the body hanging above the fire. It is hung upside down and it is swaying slightly. The mouth of the cave frames this tableaux in stone. I can't see the thing that uses one of our oars to poke at the body. In silhouette and dancing shadows, I can't tell which of my friends is hanging. I know it can't be Trent or Mark because its head is still attached. I learn that it's Jen when she starts to scream. I had hoped she was dead but she must have been unconscious, brought back into the world by the prodding.

I have been smelling her cook. I can't stay quiet, can't stop myself from being sick. Retching loudly and coughing. The smoke is burning my eyes and lungs as my body fails me. When I am able to look up again, Jen is no longer screaming. She is engulfed in flames. I can see it standing with the oar in one hand and a human leg in the other. In the brilliant light provided by what was Jen, I can see a tattoo of a skull on the calf of the leg. The monster stands waiting for me. It takes a bite from what had been Roger's leg. The skull now has a chunk of exposed muscle where its left eye socket had been.

I scramble backward, into the cave. It must know there isn't an exit because it doesn't bother to follow me. It just waits and eats. As I'm about to lose sight of it, it begins to howl. I'm around the bend in the cave and continuing to shuffle away, afraid to turn my back to the fading light. I try to tell myself that there might be an exit. That I might be close to a road, to help or salvation. I move back until I'm in full darkness again. I have turned enough subtle corners to stifle the light but not the howling. It sounds like madness and chaos and worst of all, it sounds almost human.

***

Wendigo's Woods

I'm backing up, left arm flailing behind me, when, suddenly, I'm stepping into water. My mind calls up the pamphlet Mark had showed us when he planned the trip. It had said the river was fed by underground streams and I hope more than anything I've found one. I back into the water until I can no longer touch bottom and wade back further. I think of the pamphlet again and something about a waterfall. A memory of Roger joking that we should take the canoe over it and Mark ignoring him, going on about a cave beneath the waterfall, like in the movies. I hope I'm in that cave. I hope it's going to be light soon, hope that I'll see light again, that this is all a nightmare. I wade until I hit the back of the cave. I try to feel along the wall without drowning, my right arm still useless behind me and my left knee burning with each kick. I can't find a way out. I wonder if drowning is as peaceful as I've heard.

Before I give up, I realize my eyes are closed. I don't know when I closed them, since I really hadn't been using them, but as I open them, I begin to cry. It's the kind of stupid and ugly cry that comes when you temporarily lose your mind a little. There is light in the water. A foot or two below the surface, a beautiful patch of murky water shimmers at me. It is large enough for my tiny car to drive through and I dive at it without thinking to take a breath. I almost die in the passageway, it is longer and tighter than I had thought. In the end, I find enough strength in my right arm for a final tug on the rocks that brings me back out into the world. I should have known it sooner; the rushing water had been outside the cave, not in it. I had been expecting a waterfall but it must have been another cave. I let the river carry me for a while. I'm too relieved to see the sky and taste air that doesn't smell of burning hair to think about the consequence of passing out.

***

Two hikers eventually find me on the riverbed. When the police come with the ambulance, I tell them everything. At the hospital, they tell me they found our canoe at the campsite but nothing else. They say the search dogs went crazy but no one found any evidence of the massacre. They never find the cave or the bodies of my friends.

At the police station, they show me a blurry photograph of something, it could almost be a dog or an ape or a man or a monster, racing through a forest. They show me a mugshot of a man, who is still almost a boy, with the eyes of a madman. The mugshot is twenty years older than the blurry photo and they ask me if either looks familiar.

The picture of the madman is from two states west of here; the one of the monster, from three states north. They call him, 'The Wendigo Killer'. They don't need to tell me it's happened before for me to understand it. They don't need to tell me it will happen again for me to know it.

A GOOD PRICE
Louis Rakovich

Ealdwine didn't mind the smell of the slave market. It was the dust that bothered him, and as the three of them sat in the carriage, he knew Seth and Delmar were waiting for him to pull out his handkerchief and cover his nose. Then they would pretend to follow his example, and they would curse at the thickening dust that hung like mist in the air, and they would repeat, "This weather, this weather." But they were grateful for the dust, for it allowed them to cover their noses with their dirty, perfumed handkerchiefs.

The smell reached far; they rode with it for almost twenty minutes. The dust appeared much later, and all the while in between, Ealdwine's companions sat with their faces pale and their teeth clenched. This time, he decided to spare the two some misery and pulled out his handkerchief a few minutes early.

Finally, they were at the market. The carriage stopped and Seth and Delmar stumbled out, reluctantly. Ealdwine followed. They walked in the direction of the fighter quarters, the carriage rolling slowly behind, pulling the squeaking cage wagon. Within a minute, their shoes and their black capes were covered with the white dust. Seth's hair danced in the wind.

Ealdwine lowered the crumpled handkerchief and said to him, "Cut your hair, before you start to look like your wife."

Seth let out a bitter chuckle.

Ealdwine smiled to show that he had meant no harm, and immediately, dust clung to his teeth. He spat and brought the handkerchief back to his face.

***

The fighter quarters grew quieter as they approached. Ealdwine could see the eyes of the traders pointing at him, their painted mouths stretching open into golden smiles. Some of them knew him; some merely thought he looked rich. The first few called out to him and he declined politely. He continued further into the alley between the cages, paying almost no attention to Seth and Delmar behind him. The traders shouted at their men to stand straight, and the men – tall, strong and scarred – half-complied, stuck in that twilight of ambition, equally wary of being noticed and unnoticed; for sometimes being bought was better than remaining with the trader, and sometimes much worse.

They reached the end of the street, where there stood a trader who neither called to them nor shouted at his men. He had long, black hair weaved into a thick braid, the bottom of which had been dipped in liquid gold and now gleamed dimly from under a layer of dust. His lips were painted black, and his nails, long and sharp.

"Ealdwine," he said, and threw up one limp hand.

Ealdwine lifted a few fingers in a half-wave and saw that his black glove was now a dirty gray. He came closer and nodded to the trader. "How's business?"

"Same old, darling friend, same old."

"How's the wife?"

"Better."

"I'm glad to hear that."

The trader bowed his head. "How is the Duke of Hale?"

"He's a prince now."

"Oh! The wedding finally happened?"

"Two months ago," Ealdwine said. "Three months anniversary is – what is it, Seth, leather?"

Seth shrugged.

"Well, it's something. The prince is planning a celebration. He needs fighters."

"How many?"

"Ten."

The trader smiled. His gold veneers were engraved with the image of a snake, stretched from fang-to-fang. "Two hundred each, as always," he said. "A friendly price."

Ealdwine nodded.

"Take your pick."

Ealdwine stepped closer. The fighters were tall, at least three heads taller than any man he'd ever seen outside of a cage.

"I'll take that one on the corner left," he said. "Tell the one beside him to come closer and show me his teeth."

There were forty men in the cage, and picking the best fighters wasn't easy for Ealdwine. It hadn't been easy since he realized that the biggest and least scarred weren't always the strongest. Finally, he made his last choice, urged by the weary exclamations of Seth and Delmar.

He paid the trader and with a whip in hand, the golden-teethed man led the ten fighters into the cage wagon hooked to the carriage. Ealdwine told him to give his best to his wife, and the trader passed his congratulations to the prince. The prince didn't know about the trader's existence. Ealdwine wondered whether the man's wife knew about his.

***

They went back, the carriage following behind slowly, as before. They were nearing the market's entrance when Ealdwine stopped in his tracks. He heard the carriage halt behind him.

"What is it?" asked Seth.

Ealdwine didn't answer. He approached one of the slave cages and peered inside.

The trader perked up. "Good slaves," he said. "Reliable. Fit for any type of housework."

The eagerness in this old trader's voice annoyed Ealdwine. He wiped the dust from his eyebrows and looked closer at the man sitting at the back of the cage. He appeared to be in his mid-twenties, about ten years younger than Ealdwine. His skin was pale, his hair, tar-black. He was well built, slim, not like the giant fighters.

Ealdwine threw the trader a quick look and pointed at the man. "He's interesting. Where did you get him?"

"Another trader."

"Ah. How much?"

"Fifty."

"We already have ten," said Delmar. "And this one isn't a fighter. The prince will laugh in your face if you spend his money on this."

"Not for the prince," said Ealdwine. "For me."

Delmar nodded and stepped back to stand beside Seth.

Ealdwine turned to the trader. "Get him out, I want to take a better look."

The trader pulled at the chain that was strapped to the man's wrist. "Come here." He unlocked the door. "Good posture. Good looking one, Sir, isn't he?"

Ealdwine ignored him. He studied the man, looking him up and down. He took off one glove and felt his cheek with the back of his fingers. He stroked him slowly, affectionately, then took him by the jaw and looked into his eyes. They were bright green, almost yellow. He put the length of his thumb on his lower lip.

"I'll cut you a deal," said the trader. "Forty."

Ealdwine opened the man's mouth. All his teeth were broken, as if he had been chewing stone. Only sharp stumps about half the length of healthy teeth remained. He put his other hand on the back of the man's head and kissed him softly, cautiously, studying his reaction. The man didn't resist. Ealdwine let go.

"Thirty five," he said.

A Good Price

They rode for two hours before dark, and for one hour after. Seth and Delmar had been complaining for twenty minutes when they finally reached the rest stop. Ealdwine let them run to fill their mouths with pastries and beer at the inn, while he and the driver went to water the horses and park the carriage and the cage wagon in the shed.

The inn consisted of a few, separate, one-story buildings. There was the eatery; two shared rooms, one for the servants and one for low ranking men such as Seth and Delmar; the baths, where the latter could wash up; and private rooms – simple and dirty but equipped with bathtubs of their own – for Ealdwine and his ilk.

He joined Seth and Delmar at their table. The driver went to feed the fighters and then came to sit with the drivers of the other guests.

A girl came and brought Ealdwine his meal. Delmar coaxed her to sit on his lap and fed her small bits of sweet pastry as though she were a bird. Seth, who was a newlywed, averted his gaze and tried to strike up a conversation with Ealdwine, but Ealdwine's heart wasn't in it. He finished his meal quickly, then snapped his fingers in the air and waited for another girl to approach.

"Bring two beer mugs to my room," he said. "And a few of those round, sweet things. And draw a bath." He finished his beer as she left, and turned to his companions. "All right, I'll see you tomorrow morning."

He approached the driver's table and tapped the man on the shoulder. "When you're done here, bring the new man to my room."

***

The girl was there when Ealdwine came through the door – kneeling by the bathtub and checking the heat of the water with

81

her elbow. He took off his gloves, his cape and his jacket, and began to take off his vest when she stood up and unbuttoned the collar of her blouse.

He laughed. "What are you doing?"

She didn't answer.

"Are you done with the bath?"

She nodded. He gave her a coin and sent her away.

He watched the dust spread across the surface of the water. It was dark now, not at all white, as it had seemed on his clothes. He sunk his head under the water and washed the dirt off his hair. He was looking forward to returning to Hale, where there was no dust, only dry, yellow grass and tall evergreen trees.

There was a knock on the door.

"I have the slave," said the driver's voice.

"Come in."

They entered, the chain clasped tight in the driver's grip.

"Where should I tie him?"

Ealdwine looked at the man. "Are you going to try to run away?"

"No."

"You can untie him, then."

"Are you sure?"

"You heard him. Sit him down by the table."

The driver took the chain off the man's hand and bid Ealdwine good night. The man sat staring at the food and the drink in front of him.

"You can eat it," said Ealdwine. "It's for you."

He scrubbed the remaining dust off of himself while the man ate, and finally stood and wrapped himself in a large, white towel. It stained with gray where it touched him.

"Things will be much cleaner in Hale," he said. "How's the food?"

"Good enough. A little sweet for my taste. Beer is good."

The man's frankness made Ealdwine smile. "That's good." He sat down on the bed, two feet away from the bath. "Strip and get in the tub."

The man did as he was told, removing his dirty, torn clothes and stepping into the water. He washed himself slowly, without any apparent eagerness to get clean.

"You don't mind the dust?" Ealdwine asked.

"Not very."

"Well, there won't be any dust in Hale. That's good enough, come here."

"In a moment. I want to say something."

"All right."

"I'm grateful that you bought me."

"I'm glad. Come here."

"I'm not finished. I'm grateful that you bought me, because you seem like a reasonable man. And reasonable men, like money. Do you like money?"

Ealdwine wiped the steam from his face. "Sure."

The man leaned over the edge of the tub and reached for his clothes. He produced something small and gold from one of the pockets and tossed it to Ealdwine – a signet ring bearing the customary wheat sheaf and purse of a merchant family's crest.

"What is this?"

"My parents are very rich," the man said. "There was a celebration in town one night, and I went there dressed like a common man to not call attention to myself. And as I was leaving to go back to our family estate, I was ambushed, hit over the head. I went down and woke up in a cage."

"Why did you wait to be sold to show someone the ring?"

"The first trader was a deranged brute of a man, always muttered to himself and screamed in some language I didn't know. To be honest, I was afraid of him. The second one was old and stupid, and poor for a trader. I figured he would just sell the ring and consider himself lucky. But you're a reasonable man."

"What do you want?"

"My family lives on the other side of the old grove. A five-hour walk from where we are now, at most. They would pay you for helping me return."

"How much?"

"At least enough to buy a hundred fighters. Maybe more."

"Twenty thousand?"

"Yes."

"The old grove is trouble."

"No trouble. I've walked through it hundreds of times."

"Animals and drifters. And stories of people never coming back."

"They're just stories. I wouldn't have taken you for a superstitious man."

"I'm not." Ealdwine paused and looked around the room. "All right. Your family can buy you from me for twenty thousand. Dry yourself and get dressed. You can sleep on the cot in the corner."

The man reached for another towel lying by the tub and stood up. "You aren't afraid I'll kill you in your sleep?" he asked.

Ealdwine let out a contemptuous little snort. "No."

***

When morning came, he took a bag of dried beef, two skins of water, and one of Delmar's pistols.

"I have some business to take care of," he said. "You two deliver the fighters. Tomorrow I'll take a horse and join you in Hale by evening."

"What business?" asked Seth.

Ealdwine opened his mouth to say, "I found a golden goose," but stopped, and said instead, "Business. Just business."

Soon, he and the man were on their way to the grove.

***

The grove was a wasteland. Charred, black trees stood naked on dry grass, the thinner of the branches so fragile they crumbled at the slightest touch. And the grass was not Hale's dry grass – long and golden like a woman's hair. It was short and gray, mixed with ash and dirt and poisonous weeds. Only up above the grove was green, at the tops of the trees where the fire of long ago hadn't reached. The layer of leaves cast its shadow on the ground, and the place was dim even in the morning hours, as Ealdwine and the man made their way through it.

Ealdwine had spent the first hour pointing Delmar's pistol at the man's legs, but eventually calmed down and put the weapon in its holster. The man didn't seem as though he were about to run.

"Why did your family build their house so close to this grove?" Ealdwine asked. "Such an ugly place."

The man shrugged. "It was a long time ago."

"Then, weren't they afraid of the old stories?"

"I think the stories started after they came here."

A large spider crossed Ealdwine's path. He stepped on it and watched the dark blue spill out of its bloated belly. "Old family," he said.

"Yes," said the man. "And yours?"

"The Ealdwines are an ancient clan. My father, may he rest in peace, told me we came to Hale around the same time as the prince's ancestors. I don't know if it's true."

The man stepped over a burnt log and Ealdwine followed.

"You work for the prince, don't you?"

"Yes."

"What do you do?"

"I'm in charge of the games. Men fighting to the death, wild animals ripping each other's guts out. The prince likes to watch them, but he has no clue how to run one. Where to get the best fighters, how to pair them. Oh, speaking of which – your grove."

The man stopped in his tracks and looked back at Ealdwine.

"Keep walking. The prince wanted to send me there, once. He'd heard some tales about wild animals living here, or magical creatures or some such nonsense, and thought we could catch one for the games."

"Did you?"

"No, of course not. I wasn't riding to this hellhole to be killed by some drifter while chasing an animal no one's seen."

"Some drifter could kill you?"

"No." He made a half-smile, flashing only his upper teeth. "I was speaking figuratively."

"And the prince didn't mind?"

"The prince is not an unintelligent man. He recognizes when he's out of his element. I don't tell him how to run his county and he doesn't tell me – careful!"

Ealdwine leaped toward the man and pulled him backward. They fell to the ground. A large, burnt branch landed a few inches away from their feet with a loud thud.

The man's head rested on Ealdwine's chest. Ealdwine could feel the pulsations of his fragmented breathing, and the frantic beating of his heart. He let his own head drop back on the grass and waited for a few seconds before pushing the man off and sitting up.

"Are you all right, no missing pieces?"

The man let out a short, nervous laugh. "Thank you."

Ealdwine took out his flask, engraved with a detailed scene of sailors being dragged underwater by rabid, sharp-teethed mermaids, and handed it to the man. "Thank your rich parents."

The man gulped. "So, you wouldn't have pulled me if not for the reward money?"

Ealdwine considered the question. "Sure I would. But you'd have been of a different use to me then."

"And the people who aren't of any use to you?"

"A smart man can find something to do with almost any person. Come on, let's go."

But the man remained seated on the ground. "I think I need a moment," he said.

Ealdwine tapped on his shoulder. "It's just a branch. Come on, we'll find a spot with less trees and have lunch."

They walked for about half an hour before reaching a clearing and settling down on a large rock.

"Only water and beef?" the man asked.

A Good Price

Ealdwine bit off a chunk of meat and chewed it loudly. "This is an adventure. What did you expect, a marinated duck of some sort? Cake?" He smiled. "Quit your whining, it's good beef."

"How come you're in such a good mood?"

"Thinking about what a useful purchase you'll have ended up being. Good thing that branch didn't break your head in half. Terrible luck for your parents to have their son kidnapped and then killed by a tree on his way home. Are you an only child?"

"No."

"At least. Many brothers and sisters?"

"Lots."

Ealdwine took another bite. "Your father can't keep his hands off your mother?"

The man didn't answer.

"All right, good for them." Ealdwine stood up and wiped his hands on his pants. "You ready to go?"

***

They walked. Slowly, the scenery changed. Ealdwine hadn't noticed it at first – the grove was the same grove, the trees the same trees. But the changes began to pile up, and suddenly he saw them all at once – remnants of bonfires, bits of cloth scattered on the grass, bones half-buried in the dirt.

"There were people here," he said.

The man shrugged. "Drifters."

"Maybe."

They went onward, and for a while, Ealdwine watched the man and almost forgot of the unpleasant hints of human activity around them. Then he saw the skull. It was barely half whole – the cap and one cheekbone were missing, as if someone had smashed them off with a rock. Soon after, he saw half a thighbone leaning on a burnt tree stump.

"What's going on here?" he asked. "Why are there bones lying around?"

"I don't know," said the man.

A branch broke in the distance and fell to the ground. Something beside it rustled, and then moved. Ealdwine drew his gun and came closer.

An old man lay on the grass, his torn coat almost the same color as the dirt and the weeds. He lifted his head and looked at them with round, white eyes.

"People," he said, his voice weak and raspy. "Don't shoot." He stood up and stumbled in their direction. "Don't shoot," he repeated. "They're animals."

Ealdwine lowered his gun. "Who?"

The old man approached. He was barefoot, his toes bloody stumps.

"Animals bit your toes off?" Ealdwine turned to the young man, "You said the grove was safe."

"It is."

The old man took a step forward. He was three feet away now. "Help me," he said. And then he took another step. His eyes narrowed. His breathing became louder. "You," he whispered.

And before Ealdwine could grasp what was happening, the old man took a leap – his bloody feet suddenly filled with some newfound strength – and landed on the young man, pushing him to the ground. With his bony fists, he punched him in the face – once, twice, three times. Finally, Ealdwine snapped out of the trance of surprise that had come over him and stepped toward the attacker, grabbed him by his long, tangled hair, and pulled him off. He pushed the gun against the back of the old man's head and fired. The body grew heavy. He released his grasp of the hair and let it drop to the ground.

"A mad drifter," he said. "There's nothing worse. Are you all right?"

The man was lying on his back, covering his face with his hands. Ealdwine knelt by his side and parted his fingers to reveal a bleeding nose. He poured some water on his face, and the blood washed down his cheeks. He grunted as Ealdwine touched him.

"Cut it out, you're all right. It's not broken. Goodness, man, it'll be a wonder if I get you to your family in one piece." He smiled and slapped him lightly on the cheek. "Come on."

The man sat up. "Let's just go back," he said.

"Back? Don't talk nonsense. On we go, come on. Stand up."

***

They left the dead body behind and continued their journey. They walked side-by-side now, but the man kept quiet and evaded Ealdwine's gaze. It bothered Ealdwine that he hadn't even thanked him for saving his skin, but he distracted himself with thoughts of the celebration he'd throw, the things he'd buy, once he returned to Hale.

Half-hidden behind charred trees, a cliff appeared to their left. The man stopped.

"What's wrong?" Ealdwine asked.

There was no answer.

"Come on, the other side is not for an hour."

"We're here."

"There's no house here."

"I don't live in a house."

Ealdwine looked around. The grove was darker in the shadow of the cliff. A patch of blacker darkness peered at him through the branches – a cave. A chill ran through him.

"Then where do you live?"

"Here."

Something shifted in the dark. The deep, rough voice of a stranger said, "Son?" And presently, a man stepped out of the cave. He was tall, and his bare arms strong, but thin – bones peeking through hard, angular muscles. He must have been about fifty years old. His face bore a strange, sickly expression. Something was off in the proportions of his features, eyes too far apart, upper lip slightly askew. His clothes were rags, barely holding a tangible form, but on his neck hung a fortune of gold –

coins, rings, women's necklaces, teeth minutely ornamented with gems.

He approached the young man. "Your mother worried," he said. "Gone two weeks." He turned his face toward Ealdwine. "Is that all you brought? You said you could bring at least ten from the fair. We don't have many left."

Two more faces appeared from the darkness in the cliff. Then, two more.

"No," said the young man. "No, I was attacked. Hit me on the head, sold me to a slave trader."

"This one?"

"No, some others. He helped me. Helped me get back here."

The father stepped closer to his son. "We've all missed you," he said. He spoke slowly, dragging out each sound. "This one helped?"

"Yes."

"Why?" He left his son's side and approached Ealdwine. "Why did you help him? What did he promise you?"

"Nothing," Ealdwine said.

"I don't believe you. He promised you money."

"Yes."

"I know your kind. Cowards, but greedy. You didn't help my son at all, you wanted to sell him to me."

Ealdwine stepped back and bumped into something, someone. There was hot breath on his nape. The faces by the cave had tripled, and under each face hung the belongings of their prey – gold, stones, leather, colorful bits of cloth, one glass eye.

"I'm hungry," said the father. "I have wives to feed and more children than I can count."

The young man spoke. "He did help me. He saved my life, twice. He didn't have to do that."

"Twice?"

"Yes. I'll go into town again tonight, I'll bring someone else. And there's still the old merchant. We found him. He killed him."

The father sighed. "I'm sorry, son," he said.

Ealdwine reached for his gun but a hand grasped his throat. He felt the touch of a cold razor against his skin.

"I'm sorry, son," the father repeated. "But you shouldn't have brought him here if you wanted to release him."

The man looked at Ealdwine and then down at his feet. "It was the only way I could convince him to let me go."

The father smiled and an expression of something akin to relief appeared on his face. He turned back to Ealdwine. His eyes were bluer than the glass eye dangling from the neck of one of his children – a little girl. An unbearable feeling of nausea rose up from Ealdwine's guts to his nose. His vision blurred. He blinked and saw the girl clearly again, and the eye dangled on her chest, right, left, right, left.

The father's voice reached him from some far away place. "...didn't you?"

"What?"

"You bought him, didn't you?"

"Yes."

"For how much?"

Ealdwine thought of Hale. Cypresses so wide, ten men could fit in their shadow; large picnic cloths on yellow grass; the sound of people as they cheered for the lion or the tiger or the tall, scarred man armored in gold; the villagers saying, *Mr. Ealdwine, you understand what people want, your games are all I wait for each year, truly, they are.* The taste of food; the smell of beer; the touch of skin against his lips.

He heard himself say, "Thirty-five."

The leader of the clan chuckled, and Ealdwine was back in the grove. The eye had stopped its dangling. It was closer now.

"Thirty-five," he heard the voice repeat. "I'm sorry, but it seems you've paid a good price for a very interesting death."

BACKSEAT
Jay Seate

Here's how the urban legend goes: A woman stops to get gas. After paying inside, another motorist yells something as she returns to her car. She quickly climbs in and drives away. Immediately, the man starts his engine and pursues her. He blinks his lights and honks repeatedly. On the radio, the woman hears about a maniac loose in the area. Her breath catches in her chest; scared to death her pursuer is the ballyhooed maniac in a stolen vehicle. Could she be in the wrong place at the wrong time for some nut job?

The trailing car closes the distance between them. The pursuer tailgates her. She tries to outrun him, but can't. *He's going to run me off the road and then kill me*, the woman thinks. The road is slick and winding. Her car fishtails, but she can't slow down. The tires slide sideways. Panicking, she hits the brakes, sending her into a spin. The rear of the car skids ahead of the front and off the side of the road into a ditch.

Shaken, but uninjured, she sees the other car stopped on the road above. She jumps out and runs. Fear penetrates every pore of her being. Her heart pounds beneath her breastbone as she flees. A house looms nearby. She rushes up the steps and frantically pounds on the door until the homeowner opens up.

"A man's after me. He's trying to kill me!" she cries, her body cold and her movements frenzied with impending terror.

The motorist from the trailing car approaches the house as she cringes behind the homeowner. "Thank God you got out of that car, lady," her pursuer says. "When you went inside the station, a man climbed into your backseat. I did everything I could to warn you."

End of story…

***

Due to thunderheads, night had come quickly, like a cloud of black ink. It hadn't been a good day for Arlene. Everyone on her floor had left earlier, leaving his or her cubicle like insects fleeing the colony. Finally *she* was escaping. The sounds of the office and customers reverberated in her head until she faced the echoing quiet of the parking garage. She didn't know why she thought so, but something wasn't right. Maybe it had started with the disgruntled customer who'd given her a hard time earlier that day? Or maybe it was the creepy-looking maintenance man? He always gave her the once-over, but his stares had lingered a bit longer that particular afternoon, giving her the willies. Or maybe it was just because Jim hadn't tried to reach her?

Her car had been vandalized at work, once, and she'd been spooked about shadowy places ever since. Her footsteps sounded exceptionally loud against the cement tonight. Several times, she paused and glanced back to make sure there wasn't a dark shape slipping in and out from behind garage pillars or parked cars. It wouldn't be the first time her overheated imagination messed with her perceptions. She'd heard all the urban legends and sometimes it made her go a little…well…bonkers. She quickened her pace, thinking about the legend of the killer in the backseat. It had creeped her out when she'd first heard it, right after getting her driver's license at age sixteen. The worst stories were the ones you heard when you were young, she felt. Ever since, the first thing she did before climbing into her car was to check the well behind the passenger seat. *Better safe than sorry.* Once inside her car, she locked the doors and pulled out of the parking garage and into the dark and shadowy world illuminated by the car's headlights, away from the day's concerns, or so she hoped.

Concepts of the paranormal – transparent apparitions gliding around, wispy figures appearing out of nowhere – she could handle. For her, the scariest scene Hollywood ever produced was the one where some guy, or creature, slowly sits up behind a driver, ready to commit whatever terrible atrocities the script called for. *Brrrrr*. Driving home from work or play on dark nights, she fought the urge to check her rearview mirror even though she hadn't forgotten to perform her backseat ritual.

As soon as rational thought started to return, fear goosed her again with another bugaboo. Her knuckles always tightened around her steering wheel whenever she saw a hitchhiker. That icy chill wasn't the result of bad movies, however. It was birthed by an incident during her high school days. At a stop sign, a man appeared in front of her car full of chattering teenage girls. He wore only an open raincoat and a smile, a flasher posing as a hitcher. The teenagers screamed as they drove away in yammering panic.

Ever since, whenever she saw someone hitchhiking, the image of the pervert came to mind. Thinking every one of them to be a potential, hardened criminal or an escapee from the local mental institution, she turned away from the stark figures as much as possible, especially if they wore a long coat. A hitchhiker settling into her passenger seat and then giving her a look that would turn blood to ice water—that thought gave her a double *brrrrr*.

So, here she was: another dark night and another drive from town to her cozy cottage, the perfect setting to unlock a vault of scary memories. It was a drive she'd made hundreds of times without incident, but this time, the drive felt more eerie than usual. She tried to chalk it up to pressure at work, or too much of investing herself into a current relationship. She felt as if her mind was drifting, not quite in control of what she was doing, and not where her thoughts should be before going home to an empty house with its dark corners.

If her workshop of frightening thoughts weren't draining enough, wind began whipping the trees along the roadside, the late afternoon thunderheads delivering on their imposing promise. The early darkness folded into rain clouds, as the wind continued to pick up. A drizzle soon thickened. The drops spattered the windshield like prisms with stabbing colors, causing the passing lights to glare through her windshield, threatening her further.

"Perfect," Arlene whispered, just before her body took a jolt from the car bouncing over a washed-out pothole. Her throat itched like it was made of sandpaper. She reached for a water bottle in the console, but it wasn't there. "Damnit." Water, water, everywhere, but not a drop to drink.

Every now and then, an approaching pair of headlights loomed out of the rain like a maniacal phantom with blazing eyes. The road ahead had become little more than a vague blur. Even the swish of the blades against glass was chilling. *Be-ware, be-ware, be-ware*, they seemed to hum, as Arlene thought about how quickly a long, tiring day could fuck with your psyche; how rapidly fear could stab, like an icy needle in your chest. For the briefest of moments, she caught her eyes reflected in the rearview and saw the fright in them. Once fear got started, it was hard to stop, to keep it from taking hold. She felt like the last woman left on earth, thought about Janet Leigh in the film, *Psycho,* fighting the effects of rain and headlights, but the actress's horrors weren't in the car with her. They were yet to come. The air in Arlene's vehicle was suddenly stifling. A sense of suffocation fed her panic. She opened the vents to let air inside.

She needed to think happier thoughts, like when the backseat of a car had been fun – in a boyfriend's car during her college days, for instance, parked safely on campus grounds in an area known as the hot lot. A bra being unhooked by his hands, and her unzipping a fly; prospecting inside each other's clothes, had provided pleasant forms of suspense. This blast from the past gave some comfort. The memory allowed Arlene to smile, as she got closer to her destination – a needed respite, because she and Jim hadn't been getting along lately. They hadn't even talked for a couple of days. It was bad timing, because, she would like to have gone to his place, the way she was feeling. Make-up sex would certainly help to drive her goblins away.

Oh, well.

It seemed like forever before she reached her street, safe, if not as sound as she would have liked. The rain had stopped by then. That was something, anyway. No hitchhiker, no moans from the backseat. The neighborhood looked peaceful enough. It was the current version of the American dream, where homeowners happily waved to each other across hedges on bright sunny days. She relaxed at the sight of her porch light powered, not by human hands, but by a $12.99 automatic timer purchased at the local Target, a beacon in the dark to reassure her. It would be nicer to have a friend waiting.

Lights flickered within houses up and down the block, showing signs of life she suddenly envied. A man stood on the street corner in a jogging suit, not a raincoat, thank goodness. A neighbor lady was fetching her dog from her yard to stop its yapping at the jogger. Normal enough activities, but her anxiety still lingered. She was unable to ignore the feeling that something was about to happen. Only one course of action when she felt this way: to do nothing more than wash her face, take a sleeping pill, and climb into bed, sadly, alone.

Arlene's headlights swept into her driveway. She pressed the remote. The door rumbled open and she pulled into her garage. She shut off the ignition switch and listened; nothing but the sound of the engine clicking as it cooled. With a sigh of relief, she climbed out of her car, trusting in an uneventful night, but knowing that notions of safety could be illusionary. Leaving the garage door open for a quick getaway, she moved forward with her nightly ritual of checking inside the house; she'd been doing it for years. She opened the door leading to the kitchen and flicked on a light. Something didn't feel right. A blanket of unease descended and her sense of foreboding swelled.

The house was quiet—almost too quiet, as they say—as if the wood and brickwork was holding its collective breath. She could see through the kitchen into the living room. A dim shadow stood against the far wall. Arlene's eyes bulged in their sockets as the shadow moved ever so slightly. Gooseflesh rippled up her arms. She had no pets to scurry around the house. Someone waiting inside for her was the third scariest thing, queuing up behind a car's backseat and hitchhikers. Could fears, like disasters, come in threes?

With crushing clarity, she knew the shadow was unquestionably human. No wonder she'd had a premonition of danger—a warning. She put her hands over her mouth to hold in a scream. A cramp knifed through her bowels. The tendrils of hair on the back of her neck felt like crawling spiders, but she didn't freeze. Refusing to let paralysis grip her, Arlene's brain devolved into instinctive movement, for, at the core, everyone is a survivalist. She turned on her heel and bolted back toward her vehicle. *Thank God* she hadn't yet closed the garage door. *Thank her lucky stars* for her paranoia – her nightly, ceremonial neurosis. It was almost as if she'd been preparing for this quick getaway her entire life.

The thing that wasn't in the backseat or alongside the road had become the thing in her house. With keys in hand, she threw her purse into the passenger seat, fired up the sensible, good-on-gas, economy car, and quickly backed down the drive and into the street. Though her heart was in her throat, she functioned smoothly. Barely glancing back at her house, she sped away.

After driving a few blocks to what she considered a safe distance, she pulled over and tried to quiet the roaring in her head.

Safe.

The adrenaline rush was too strong to contemplate what had happened. The street she'd stopped on was mostly dark, barely exposed by a reluctant moon. She fished her cell phone out of her purse. The little screen lit the darkness with its blue light, displaying a plethora of screen choices. She punched in 911, reported an intruder inside her house, and gave her address. She sat quietly for a moment, giving the police time to respond. She would call Jim. She could tell him what happened and drive to his place. Everything would sort itself out in his arms.

Her phone suddenly purred and vibrated in her hand. She punched the talk button.

"Hello?"

Jim's voice. "Arlene? What the hell? Where the heck did you go?"

"What?"

"Why did you take off? I was waiting in the dark for you. I have a surprise."

"Waiting in the dark for me?"

"Well, I have a key, you know, and I wanted to make up by surprising you with a token of affection—*me*."

Much like a pot of boiling water, removed from a burner, Arlene's breathing slowed. Her shoulders relaxed, allowing the weight of fear to fall from them, as her emotions stabilized. She felt both relieved and embarrassed, just as the headlights of a patrol car made her squint as it passed, on the way to her house.

"Jim, I thought you were..." She could almost see him smiling, that kind of smirk men get when they are thinking about how silly women can be. "If you're undressed, you'd better put your clothes on. The cops are on their way. I called 911."

"Jesus, Arlene!"

"I'll be there in a minute. Please don't get yourself shot in the meantime." She closed the phone and imagined Jim sheepishly coming from her house to face a police officer. She guessed he would have some 'splainin' to do, but afterwards, it would be all right – a bizarre ending to a difficult day. She would tell him about her fear of backseats and hitchhikers, and he would make her forget everything, when they climbed into her bed. The sweet anticipation of what would follow produced a sigh.

Arlene turned on the ignition. The engine caught and purred. At the same time, the car creaked slightly. Her head jerked up and she peered out the driver's side window, seeing nothing but the dark street. Then she heard a muffled thumping sound...like a fist against the inside of a coffin lid...or...feet stomping in the well of the backseat. She glanced into her rearview mirror as habit dictated. A figure sat there, the face obscured by shadows and a hood pulled up on the jacket – a specter from her deepest fear, in the flesh.

Her terror searched for answers. *How? When?*

Answers. *Man (Jogger) on corner. Open garage door. Waiting for opportunity. In the wrong place at the wrong time.*

Arlene caught a gamey whiff of the man's sweat and her mouth opened to scream, but all that came out was a stifled croak, as her airway was cut off by strangling hands. Her keys dangled harmlessly from the ignition. No Good Samaritan in this scenario. No safe haven to prevent her worst nightmare from becoming what urban legends feed on.

End of story…

NIGHT FEEDS
Kris Ashton

We pulled up outside the hotel in Blasten and met at the hood of our rental car. I put my arm around Jane's shoulders; she kept her arms folded. We both looked up at the hotel, at its splitting weatherboard façade and balcony that ran the length of its frontage. Some balusters were missing from the balcony rail, making it look like an old man's grin. Two opaque windows did nothing to dispel the image of an ancient face. Until that moment, we had seen only photos of it.

"That's our hotel," I said.

Jane nodded. It was one of two reactions she now had: a flat nod, yes, or a lethargic shake of the head, no. I had hoped seeing the hotel in the splintered flesh might provoke a more fervent reaction. The nod bleached what little color had seeped into my day.

"Well, I guess we'd better go pick up the keys and see what we've bought."

Gravel crunched beneath the tires of our car. None of the roads in Blasten were paved; it was too remote and harbored too few residents for any local government to bother putting down tarmac. According to my research, only eight hundred and thirteen citizens permanently called Blasten home. Now it was eight hundred and fifteen.

We walked up the stoop to Miles Barrow's modest cottage and I rapped on the door. I glanced at my watch and could not believe it was after eight p.m. The sun's warm face floated two or three heads above the horizon and would not set again for a week or so. That had been part of Blasten's appeal: no long nights where Jane and I tossed and writhed and visited the toilet half a dozen times between us. What I would miss least in those small, despairing hours was the crinkle and pop of a blister pack, a declaration that Jane had given up and resorted to a sleeping pill. I had tried the pills myself, but they left me feeling dazed and dried out, which was worse than the grit-eyed apathy that came from an hour or two of real sleep.

Miles opened the door. He gave us a car salesman grin. "Todd and Jane," he effused, pointing to each of us in turn and then shaking our hands. "Glad to see you made it in one piece. No trouble with the roads?"

"Once I figured out the truck drivers were all insane it was smooth sailing," I said.

Miles laughed and clapped me on the shoulder. "You're not wrong there. Will you come inside for a cup of coffee or a beer?"

I was already stoked like a locomotive thanks to the four coffees I'd had on the road. A beer sounded all right, but I knew Jane would refuse and just sit in a corner with a blank expression. That was awkwardness I could do without.

"Thanks, but we really want to check out the hotel. You know, see what we've bought."

"Understand totally," Miles said, raising a hand, "I'm a businessman myself. I hope you folks can make a go of that place. It's been genuinely depressing watching it go to wrack and ruin. I'll fetch the keys for you."

He disappeared inside. I flipped up the collar on my jacket; the sun was warm but the wind was picking up and it seemed to be infused with dry ice. Jane put her hands in her pockets and hunched her shoulders.

"Here they are," Miles said, brandishing a huge key ring. "They all look the same, so I've labeled the ones for the main doors. You'll have to work out the rest for yourselves. To be honest, I didn't expect to sell the place so quickly." He passed the key ring to me. Its weight corresponded to its size. "That's a piece of Blasten's history you've got right there. When you get the place up and running, let me know. I'll be your first customer. I take my whisky neat."

"Whisky, neat," I repeated. "Thanks, Miles. We'll see you around."

"No doubt about that," Miles said. "Blasten's a small place and liable to get smaller if the environmentalists get their way. You wouldn't think a town this small would show up on their radar, but... Ahh, pardon me, folks. Sometimes I get up on my soapbox. You two have a look around and get yourselves settled. Tomorrow we can finalize the paperwork. How does that sound?"

I shook Miles' hand and told him it sounded fine. Jane's hands remained in her coat pockets and if she said goodbye I didn't hear it. We trudged back to the car, our eyes crow-footed against the sun.

I grabbed my sunglasses from the car's console and then drove us back to the hotel. We got out and ascended the two stairs to the porch, timber creaking beneath our feet. It might have been old, but it sounded and felt solid. As we stood at the double-door entrance, I stamped my feet. "No termites here, at least. Too cold."

Jane had nothing to add.

***

We were in our thirties when Jane and I began trying for a baby. The modern malady: work first, life second. Six barren months later, it became clear life had no intention of adhering to our schedule. Jane's period stopped being a minor inconvenience and became, instead, a bright red disaster delivered in monthly installments. Sex, for the first time in our lives, became drudgery, a chore completed along with the washing up and the vacuuming. But worse was the fortnight that followed, as we waited in hopeful anxiety to see if those dreaded painters would take up residence again.

When Jane turned thirty-three we called time on our robotic lovemaking and saw a fertility specialist. Tests delivered a double-whammy: low sperm count and cystic ovaries. We invited science into our bedroom and began IVF.

Then came the miscarriages.

The first one disappointed us, the second (which held for three months) devastated us and the third left us in numb despair. Just before we tried for the fourth and final time, Jane brought up the subject of adoption. Outwardly, I brushed off the idea – "Let's just see how this one goes," or something equally inane – but inwardly, I baulked. If I couldn't stand our friends' kids most of the time, why the hell would I bring a stranger's child home to stay?

I don't believe either of us thought the fourth embryo would go to term. The week after we learned Jane was pregnant with Stephan, I bought a cross and chain at a jeweler. By then, I was prepared to explore any avenue, even faith. We spent nine months waiting for something to go wrong (even though from the sixth month the obstetrician assured us we were almost certainly out of the woods). When Jane's water broke, I bundled her into the car and drove to the hospital in a stupor. I only believed it was real when Stephan came into the world and told us, at the top of his lungs, that all was well.

A son. We had a son.

We brought Stephan home and loved him and doted on him and fretted about him like the new parents we were. Then, early on a spring morning, I woke to find an acronym had stolen Stephan away from us. SIDS was a medical term I had heard of but never paid much attention to. I found Stephan's tiny body, blue and still, in the bottom of the cot. He was cosseted in the apple-green blanket my mother had knitted for him. I picked him up and touched the flesh of his cheek, just to be sure, but felt no warmth against my finger. I stood there with his lifeless form cradled in my arms and tried to deflect the emotions firing in. If one pierced the armor of my psyche, it would open the way to another. And another...

Jane. What words did one use when delivering such news? What phrasing could possibly soften the blow of this final gut-punch?

My feet carried me to our bedroom, where Jane still slept with a cat-like peacefulness.

A son. We had a son.

***

I fingered through the keys until I found one with a small, yellow label marked FRONT. I slotted it in the keyhole. The lock squeaked but its tumblers turned easily enough.

The doors opened outwards. I splayed them as far as they would go and then stepped in. I inhaled the hotel's scent, which made me think of old library books. In front of me was the bar, beneath which ten stools were parked. I tested one of the stools. It did not wobble or squeak. In fact, it felt as solid as a tree stump.

"Didn't expect these to still be here," I said. I touched the bar top. It was coated in a thin layer of dust and bore a century of scars, but had lost no charm for any of that. I couldn't identify the hardwood from which it was fashioned, but thought it must have cost the original owner a fortune. To the left of the bar, the oak floor bore the scuff marks of many chairs and tables, although the furniture was now absent. The bathrooms were also situated in this corner.

I ran my finger along the length of the bar. It left a dark line in its wake. The mirrored wall behind the bar caught Jane's slack-faced disinterest.

I held up my dust-coated finger. "First order of business down here."

Jane wrinkled her nose. "Gross."

I smiled. A single syllable was better than I could expect on most days.

To the right of the bar was a door labeled BASEMENT, and adjacent to that was a staircase leading up. I put one hand on the banister and extended the other to Jane. "Shall we?"

She took my hand with a limp-lettuce grip that was somehow worse than no contact at all. Our ascending footsteps sounded like a slow heartbeat.

Upstairs we found a hallway with four doors spaced out along it. Each stout, timber door had a brass number screwed onto it. Behind these doors, so Miles had explained over the phone, generations of fishermen and miners had rested their weary and booze-addled heads. I opened door one. The room's single window faced north, admitting only chancy light. Gauzy curtains, two decades beyond their prime, hung like rags either side of the window frame. My eyes took a moment to adjust, and when they did, I almost wished I were blind.

Jane was beside me and I heard her draw breath. I closed my eyes against the scene in an involuntary flinch. When I opened them again, Jane was already in the hall and making a fast line for the stairs. I could hear the strangled sobs in her throat.

"Jane," I called after her, but the call was feeble. Part of me was tired of comforting, tired of nursing her wounds when I had so many of my own. I shot a hateful look at the old crib standing in the corner. Of all the goddamned furniture that could be left behind in a hotel, why a crib? Why not a bed frame or a rocking chair or a fucking geriatric toilet seat over a chamber pot? Why did it have to be that antique monstrosity throwing bars of shadow against the wall?

I walked up to the crib and raised my foot, meaning to kick it and hopefully shatter a couple of its ribs. But all at once the rage washed out of me and left behind only crushing despair. I swallowed. It wasn't enough. I swallowed again and then drew a breath that stuttered in my throat. Before anything more could happen, I swiped my palm across the window-pane and pressed my forehead against its cool glass. The window offered a streaky view of the headland, which butted up against a cold, grey sea.

Whitecaps flecked the water while large ships, small at that distance, seemed motionless on the swell.

"What in God's name have we done?" I whispered.

Unable to stand another second in proximity to that crib, I strode – nearly dashed – from the room and slammed the door shut behind me. Something oily rose up and coated the inside of my throat. I clutched at my neck and began stumbling down the stairs, willing the strange nausea to recede.

I composed myself, for Jane's sake, before I reached the bottom of the stairs, but I needn't have bothered. She sat, cross-legged in the middle of the oaken floor, her head bowed and her hands in her lap. Her hair obscured her face in a chestnut veil.

I approached, walking softly, and then stood beside her with my hands on my hips. I opened my mouth, a fine start, but then fell dumb. What could I say? I'd been on the verge of a panic attack myself; it would be like one slightly less violent psychopath trying to counsel another.

"I heard voices," Jane said.

I licked my lips. She had spoken into her lap and her voice was muffled, so I wasn't sure I'd heard her right. "Did you say..."

She lifted her head enough that it cancelled the muffling effect. "I heard voices."

"What voices?"

"They're in the floor," she said.

It's tipped her over, I thought. *Seeing the crib has pushed her from grief into something more serious.*

"What do you mean voices in the floors?"

My wife shrugged. She continued to stare at her legs. "I heard voices."

My panic rose again. I scurried to the basement door, cowardly as a mouse, and began to pick through the jumble of keys with shaking fingers. None of the little yellow labels said BASEMENT and there were far too many keys without labels to try a process of elimination. In desperation I turned the handle. The door popped open.

Night Feeds

I stepped inside and ran my hand over the wall for a light switch. It wasn't hard to find: an old-fashioned toggle switch protruding from the center of a box. When I snapped it on, a bare bulb lit up, casting yellow light down a short flight of concrete stairs. I began stepping down, placing my palm against the cold wall to steady myself because there was no handrail.

The stairs ended at a passage, which ran away to my left. Here dangled a second bare bulb, while a third illuminated the far end of the passage. Thin, copper-colored pipes hung from the ceiling like tree roots in a cave. These, I knew, were the 'lines': pipes that would one day connect to beer kegs and send laughing juice up to the bar taps. But that was as much as I knew. Had we really believed we could run a bar without a single minute of publican's experience between us? No, we had never even got that far. I had come up with this hare-brained scheme and Jane had submitted to it – a shred of paper blown along in a wild wind.

What I remember next is thinking, *fireflies.* Two red fireflies had appeared in the half-gloom between the light behind me and the light at the far end of the keg room. They hovered there, mesmerizing, and then came towards me. Too fast. Fireflies couldn't move like—

The woman's face seemed to coalesce around the fireflies, thin-featured and beautiful but marred with strange dimples about the brow. Dark hair billowed out around a pale complexion and I understood, on some level, that I was hypnotized, a raccoon caught in the headlights of an oncoming car.

Her slight frame knocked me flat onto the concrete floor. Her lips pulled back, revealing teeth that belonged in an Alsatian's mouth. She lunged for my throat, but the collar of my fleece-lined jacket was still upturned and I felt two points of blunt pressure just below my jawbone. And I smelled her breath — not merely halitosis but the noxious fumes of something that had died and started to rot.

That stench broke the spell. I began to scream, the brainless, animal scream of a monkey in the clutches of a leopard. I grabbed her neck with both hands and pushed her face away from mine. Or, at least, I tried to; it was like grappling with a heavyweight wrestler. She snapped at my face, her teeth clicking an inch from my nose. My arms began to shake and I knew they would soon collapse at the elbows. How could she be so heavy? That was the thought that skittered through my mind between the ululations that whitewashed everything. How could a woman who appeared to weigh one hundred pounds actually weigh three hundred?

The tiny muscles at the back of my arms buckled. I shut my eyes, not wanting to see that beautiful ghost-face as it pierced the tender flesh on my neck...but I heard only a frustrated cry.

I opened my eyes to see Jane standing above me with two handfuls of the woman's hair. She pulled back on it as if reining in a runaway carthorse. "Get off him!" Jane screamed. It was the first thing she had said in three months that qualified for an exclamation mark. "Leave him alone!"

The vampire – for I knew she could be nothing else – left off her gluttonous quest for my throat and sat up, straddling me. I heard a sound like the strike of a match and then the sharp report of flesh on flesh. In my peripheral vision, I saw Jane collapse against the wall, her hands pressed to her cheek. Protruding from her balled fingers were thin tufts of raven-black hair.

I fired a punch at the woman's delicate chin, all thoughts of civil propriety evicted from my head. But she caught my fist and locked my arm against the cold floor. I tried to resist, but I might as well have been an infant. She looked at my neck, bloodlust etched across her face. A clawed hand grabbed for my collar and ripped it back, two shirt buttons popping off in the frenzy.

The vampire let out a shriek – I can only liken it to an eagle's cry, but that omits the sandpapery hiss behind it and another quality that defies words – and then she fell back, her hands shielding her face, as if to ward off flames. She wriggled away on her bottom until she backed up against the wall.

I glanced down at the crucifix nestled in my chest hair, its cheap gold making chintzy flashes under the harsh, basement light. Although I felt woozy, I scrambled to my feet and plucked the cross from its nest of hair. I held it out past my chin and stared, bug-eyed, at the vampire, who was now tucked in a small ball.

"It's blinding me!" she cried. "Put it away!"

"Like hell I will." Instead, I advanced on her, loosing the cross from around my neck and holding it before me. The vampire screamed, an ear-scalding sound from hell's deepest pits, and her exposed hand began to smoke like green leaves on a fire.

"PLEEEASE!"

She said something else, but all her hypnotic tricks were null. Now, there was only the urge to kill, to destroy something dangerous and unholy. I brought the crucifix closer, relishing what might happen when it touched that powder white skin...

"Todd, wait!"

Jane's voice cut through the kill instinct. I kept the cross where it was but permitted my eyes to roll towards my wife. She was back on her feet. Red welts striped her cheek and her blue eyes shone in her face like stars.

"Jane, stay back, honey."

"She said she has a boy."

"What?"

"I do," the vampire whimpered.

"Jane, it's a trick. You know what she is, don't you?"

Jane paid me no heed and began to pace towards the shadows at the back end of the basement. My heart groaned and sang at the same time; for while I feared for Jane's safety, I also felt joy at her sudden purpose.

"There is a boy!" Jane said, her voice ringing off the walls.

"Please don't hurt him!" the vampire said. She writhed beneath the invisible scorch of the crucifix. I licked my lips and then began to shuffle sideways, keeping my necklace trained in her direction. The wisps of smoke palling up from her skin began to thin out, but she still shielded her eyes.

I twisted my head around and peered into the gloom. Curled up against the wall was a boy of no more than seven or eight. On a quick inspection, any sane person might have assumed him dead – a small corpse too fresh for decomposition. He had his mother's pale skin, except it also had a translucent sheen – as if his very matter had gone to water. He wore what appeared to be a school blazer, its formality adding to the funereal impression. When my eyes had fully adjusted to the darkened corner, I could just make out the slow rise and fall of his ribcage.

"Watch yourself, Jane!" I called to her. "He could be playing possum."

"He's not playing possum," said the vampire. The shrillness was gone and she now sounded matter-of-fact. "If he doesn't feed, he'll soon be dead."

I turned back. Her face was averted from my cross, but she had lowered her hand. "What do you mean? He's already dead, isn't he?"

"We are *undead*," she said in a patronizing tone. "The undead are not truly alive, but they can still die. If they are touched with a crucifix, for instance. Or, if they do not feed for a long time. We have been trapped down here for more than three weeks."

"Oh, my heart bleeds," I said, taking two steps closer. She cringed back against the wall and raised her hands again. "A few moments ago, you were trying to tear my goddamned throat out."

"For him," the vampire wailed. "For my boy."

"Yeah, right."

"Todd, wait," Jane said. She left the boy's side and joined me. "Just, back off with that thing a bit, will you?"

"You can't be serious, Jane..."

"It's burning her, can't you see that?"

"I can see just fine." But I retracted the cross. The smoke and its carbonic odor began to dissipate again.

"How did you get trapped down here?" Jane asked.

"We were in the hold of a ship," the vampire said, her face still turned to the wall. "It was due to land further south, but bad weather must have forced it off course. When it docked at Blasten, the hull was damaged and crew and cargo were unloaded much earlier than expected. We...we were discovered and chased from the ship. We had only minutes to find sanctuary before the sun came up. It has stayed up ever since."

"Oh, that's dreadful," Jane said. "And your boy...?"

"He has not fed since we came down here. Neither of us has. Although I am mad with hunger, it will not kill me for some time to come. But, my boy...I think his time is almost gone."

Jane ran a hand across her mouth. "How can we help you?"

I gawped at her. "Are you completely out of your mind? Have you forgotten she just tried to kill me? To...to make me like her?"

"Todd, don't be a child. There's no sense getting angry at her. It's like getting angry at a dog. She didn't want to hurt you."

"How about I throw this cross away," I said, "and then, we'll see how much she doesn't want to hurt me."

"He's right," the vampire said sullenly. "When the hunger is this strong, it becomes a reflex, like blinking your eyes."

"Think I'm a child now, Jane?"

"She's just being honest. What can she do with you waving that thing around, anyway?"

"Oh, Jesus," I said, shaking my head. "I don't believe this."

"There must be some way we can help you," Jane said.

"Only your blood can save my boy. There is nothing else you can do to help us."

"Well, that sounds pretty cut and dried to me, Jane," I said. "You want to be like them?"

"What if...what if we fetch some blood for you? We could search for a dog or a cat—"

"A defamatory myth," the vampire said. "We cannot consume the blood of animals. It must be human blood."

Jane was not to be discouraged. "We can donate some blood. You know, just a little nick on the finger or something like that?"

"The blood cannot touch the air or it becomes stale. And if the boy's saliva enters your bloodstream..."

"Man, this stuff is complicated," I said. "It's almost like someone is telling you *not to do it*, Jane."

But those lights were dancing in her eyes and she wore an expression I hadn't seen in months – perhaps even a year. My wife had set her mind to solving a problem and would not stop until she found the answer.

I sighed and put a hand on her arm. "It's only another few days until the sun starts to set again. Her boy will probably survive that long. Hell, he's a vampire – he'll outlive both of us." I looked past the cross, which was still trained on the vampire like a rifle sight. "We won't tell anyone about you. When it's safe, you can make your escape."

I had progressed from prey, to interrogator, to diplomat. The vampire said nothing.

"That's not good enough," Jane said.

"What are you talking about? A minute ago you were ripping her hair out!"

She ignored me. To the vampire, she said, "Do you think your son could survive a few days?"

The vampire shook her head.

"Well, of course she's going to say that. She wants to make a meal of the both of us."

"There must be something we can do."

"There's nothing, Jane. Unless you want to spend the rest of your unnatural life like her."

The basement fell silent. It felt colder than ever down there, as if our collective breath had lowered the temperature instead of raising it. Jane bit her thumbnail, as she always did when she was trying to cut through a knotty problem.

I considered handing her the crucifix and telling her to come find me when she was done (if she didn't have puncture marks on her throat), when she spoke.

"I might have an idea."

She told us the idea.

I made a gagging sound and said, "For God's sake, Jane, you can't be serious."

The vampire said, "It could work. I don't know."

"Could it be done without...you know. Making me into one of you?"

"If there is no broken skin, you should not be infected."

Jane bit her lip. "I'm willing to try," she said.

"But I'm not willing to let you!" I cried. "You're not thinking straight, Jane! You're grieving, we both are, but this—"

"I know what I'm doing."

"How can you possibly? Even *she* isn't sure it's going to work," I said, jabbing the cross at the vampire and making her wince anew.

"I'm doing it," Jane said. "Want to try and stop me?"

We both knew the answer to that. If I tried to stop her, it would turn into a wrestling match and I would have to lower the cross. A two-course buffet, *ala human,* would ensue.

"If you turn, I'll kill you," I said. "All three of you."

My wife looked me up and down and then turned her back to me. She kicked off her shoes, unbuckled her belt and dropped her jeans. Her thermal underwear – a garment foreign to us before our move to Blasten – followed. Her underpants were last and she stepped out of them in her woolen socks, which she kept on (a sensible measure that only made the situation more bizarre).

"Get that thing out of her face, Todd," Jane said. "She needs to be able to speak to her boy."

The sight of my wife naked from the waist down and wearing such an earnest expression was almost as hypnotic as the vampire's firefly eyes had been. I shuffled backwards, enough to withdraw the worst of the glare that only the vampire could see. She got to her feet with a regal litheness that made my flesh creep and my loins tingle. I managed to make some words stumble over my numb lips.

"Try anything and you're dead."

"Hush now, Todd," my wife said.

They approached the vampire boy, two mothers, one lately bereaved. The vampire crouched to her child and rolled him over so he was on his back, his peaked face staring up at the curve of half-light on the basement ceiling.

"Don't bite," the vampire told her son. He made no response I could discern, but his mother stood up again and nodded at Jane.

My wife stepped forward and stood over the boy, her legs a little more than shoulder width apart. Then she dropped to her knees and gently lowered herself until her lips met his.

The foot of the crucifix dug into the heel of my palm. I later found a square blood blister on that spot, but at that moment, I felt almost nothing. I was waiting for the sudden click of sharp teeth, for the scream, for the flow of blood and the feeding frenzy.

What came, instead, were suckling noises.

I wanted to be sick to my stomach; my wife connected in such an unnatural union with a tiny, undead devil. But those suckling sounds were the most natural thing in the world.

The vampire's mother stood beside them, her hands clasped to her bosom and a small smile curling those blood-red lips.

"Thank you," she said.

ROUGHER THAN THE REST
Adrian Ludens

The gypsy with the colorful headscarf and gold rings encircling her thumbs warned me. She looked me straight in the eye and revealed her prediction for my demise: cholera. I gave her a second, more valuable coin and said a few words of my own. She arched one black brow as she considered my request. Then she nodded.

Samuel, my husband, burst into the tent, just as she finished her ministration. His hand snapped onto my wrist like a bear trap. A thrill rose up within me; he was angry. Having an argument with my husband usually involved us making up later, rough and tumble, on the bed in our cabin.

"Josephine! I told you not to waste our hard-earned money on this gypsy trash," my husband growled. His good eye blazed. "It's all claptrap."

The prominent bulge in his pants betrayed his enjoyment of the Hoochie Coochie girls dancing in an adjacent tent, an attraction I knew was not free, but I held my tongue. Instead, I wrested free from his grasp. Samuel reached for me again and the Fortune Teller snatched his hand. She twisted it palm up and gasped at what she saw. The gypsy spat into his palm.

"*Lupos!* The brute will be unleashed!"

I looked up in time to see her cross herself.

Samuel yanked me from my seat at the tiny, fabric-covered table and pulled me out into the night. The cool air slapped me across the face. I wondered if Samuel would do the same. My husband dropped my hand and wheeled to face me. His bloodshot blue eye looked like a frozen pond surrounded by a raging wildfire. I flinched. Then his gaze softened and he pressed his lips to mine.

"I'm no brute, Josie," he murmured. "You know that."

One of us let out a muffled sob, but we were so enmeshed that I hesitate to say which of us had done it. We turned and hurried to the livery where our gray gelding, Smokey, waited with our wagon.

***

The gypsy woman in the traveling carnival we'd visited that evening wasn't the only one from whom I'd heard the dire proclamation of cholera. Earlier in the afternoon, while Samuel gathered supplies for our homestead at the dry goods store, I made up an excuse about looking elsewhere for some special fabric for new curtains. Instead, I walked to Doc Cortney's. Samuel did not know it, but I got the bad news there first. The frequent trips I'd been taking to the outhouse and my painful leg cramps helped Doc make his diagnosis. The man of science and the woman of mysticism were in agreement. I had cholera, and precious little time left.

***

Samuel turned and spat in the dust as we journeyed home in the buckboard wagon. "I can't believe you wasted hard-earned money on that pretender," he scoffed. Samuel gripped the reins and urged Smokey toward home. The full moon lit up his scowling face. "Cholera, she says? She's wrong—dead wrong! But that's what you get for bein' foolish, Josephine."

I wasn't sure if my husband's anger stemmed from me spending money against his wishes or from the Fortune Teller's grim prediction. I sought to soothe and distract him.

I recalled his evident enthusiasm for the Hoochie Coochie girls at the carnival. I felt a tingle awakening between my hips at the memory of his arousal. My body seemed to throb with insistent heat. I knew how tempestuous Samuel could be during our intimate moments.

Our bouts of rough lovemaking never failed to thrill me. For Samuel's part, they seemed to exorcise his anger. I often woke the next morning to find my body bruised and scratched, but always felt a warm sense of satisfaction. Samuel doted on me; meek as a lamb and eager to please me and make me laugh. The love we shared was often wild and untamed, yes, but it satisfied our hearts. Some claim their love to be "tougher than the rest." I would use another word: *rougher.*

I reached into his wool pants and found his cock. I nuzzled his sunburned neck and stroked him to firmness. I'd milked cows as a girl and had used that experience to perfect a technique quite pleasing to my husband. Samuel freed one hand from the reins to lift my gingham skirt. I stood, holding onto his shoulder for balance. He pulled down my bloomers and I straddled him, felt him penetrate me. I watched the dust rise from the path behind us. Samuel pushed his boots against the floor of the buckboard, swiveling his hips to accentuate our merger. The jouncing of the buckboard along the path did the rest. The wagon wheels vibrated over a stretch of road turned into a washboard by rainwaters and I gave myself over to the pleasure as it peaked within me.

My head swam. Tiny, red lights peppered my vision. At first my eyes could not refocus in the darkness, but when they finally did, I thought they played tricks. Roiling shadows—not trail dust—kept pace behind the jouncing wagon. The tiny, red lights stayed with us as well. Dozens of them, in pairs, seemed to glide along behind us. More shadows raced alongside. My heart raced along with them. I realized each silent shadow contained a pair of glittering eyes. At last, I comprehended the truth:

Wolves.

I could not breathe. Samuel continued to thrust himself into me, oblivious. I knew he had an old squirrel gun stashed somewhere in the wagon, but I doubted it would do anything to scare off an entire wolf pack. I tried to speak but could not find my voice. Straddling my husband, my skirt pushed up my bare thighs, I felt exposed – vulnerable. I clutched at his sleeve, too late.

One of the wolves near the front separated itself from the pack and leaped up at Smokey's throat. Our horse tried to rear up but got his forelegs tangled and went down, head first.

The buckboard jerked—hard. I flipped over the front of the moving wagon, ass over teakettle, as my Uncle Oren used to say. I felt the reins entangle me for a moment, and then they tore loose from my husband's grasp and my descent continued. I crashed into the dirt in front of a rolling wheel, felt it press down on my neck.

The sound in my ears was like a gunshot.

I had the strangest idea, then, that the moon was an enormous silver eye. It reminded me of Samuel's bad eye, the one he had lost one night while we made love. I thought the moon must have gotten tired of watching our little drama unfold because it dropped a lid over itself and sent everything into darkness, taking me with it.

***

"Josephiiiiine!"

The word was drawn out in a shrill howl. Several of the wolves seemed to mock him with howls of their own.

"Josie! I'm comin'. Get back, you mangy sonsabitches!"

Samuel. I opened my eyes and rose. He ran toward me, panting, intending to save me from the wolves.

The moonlight had returned. I wondered if it had gone away at all. In the silvery gleam, I saw trail dust billowing around like smoke. A few of the wolves tore into poor Smokey. Their snapping jaws shimmered, coated with wet gore.

The rest of the wolves circled Samuel. My husband held the squirrel gun like a club. He hadn't even had time to load it. He swung but the wolves shrank back out of harm's way.

The gun slipped from his hands and Samuel seemed to forget it as he staggered toward me. The wolves moved with him; kept him surrounded. The largest wolf separated itself from the pack and crept up behind Samuel, close enough to be his shadow. My husband did not notice. He kept on mumbling his apologies. Samuel now stood so close that I could see the tears blazing trails down his flushed and dusty cheeks.

Love for my husband surged within me. I stepped forward, needing to hold him in spite of—or perhaps because of—our dire situation.

Samuel stepped forward. He passed right through me.

The lead wolf stood up, a horrifying parody of a man.

I turned to see a figure wearing a calico dress, just like mine, crumpled in the dirt. Samuel fell to his knees beside her.

"Josie, I'm sorry. I'm too late," he muttered. "I'm so damned sorry."

The wolf towered over my husband. I tried to scream. No sound came.

The gigantic wolf-creature pounced on Samuel, enveloping him from view. I don't know if his shriek was of pain, anger or sorrow. Perhaps it was a mixture of all three. The wolf clenched my husband's forearm between its massive jaws and shook him. Samuel flailed like a cloth doll and then skidded through the dust and into the tall grass.

"Murderers!" Samuel's voice cracked. He scrambled to his feet and dashed away through the field. The wolves stood watching him go.

The members of the pack made a quick and bloody feast of my empty shell. To take my mind off the carnage, I looked up at the silver disc in the sky. This time, it reminded me of the second coin I'd given the Fortune Teller.

I saw myself back in her tent, pleading for a miracle. The last words the gypsy had said to me, before Samuel burst in, came back to me. She'd placed her left thumb on the center of my forehead and had intoned:

"Every full moon. For love."

***

There came a period of darkness, of nothingness.

Gradually, I became aware of my surroundings. Darkness birthed a silver orb above. Familiar colors slowly asserted themselves around me, though they remained muted in shades of gray. I savored the scent of our lilac bushes, stronger in my nostrils now than ever before. The coolness of the night breeze ran invisible fingers through my hair and along my bare skin. The hypnotic, abrasive song of the katydids accompanied my arrival.

The moon, cream-colored and full, hovered high above, shining its soft light on my surroundings. It thrilled me to see our homestead, our cozy little cabin. The blades of grass pushed back against the soles of my feet as I hurried forward. I panted with exertion—and anticipation. Soon, I would feel my husband's rough, but loving touch. I vowed to relish our time together, to make the most of it.

I saw the telltale flame of a candle burning in a window. It brought to mind the night my husband suffered his injury. Samuel had been in a foul mood; the wheat harvest had been less—much less—than expected, and several head of livestock had taken ill. Times were tougher than normal. I had wanted to treat him to something special, something extraordinary. Though he never blamed me, the fault was mine. I paused near our cabin and closed my eyes, lost in reverie.

***

I lit two beeswax candles. Samuel allowed me to tie his wrists to the bedposts with rawhide reins. I climbed atop him and rode him as if he were a horse facing forward, sidesaddle, backward. After teasing him for the better part of an hour, I eased myself off of his manhood and reached for the candles. I took one in each hand. Samuel looked on, curious. I straddled his chest, facing away, so that my husband had a full view of most intimate areas.

Then I took one of the candles and inserted it where his shaft had been moments before. Samuel groaned, obviously pleased with the view, but also reacting to the hot wax that dripped onto his skin. I reached back with the second candle, intending to push it into the puckered orifice that had heretofore only welcomed the tentative explorations of my own fingers. It proved to be more of a challenge than I had anticipated. In my attempts to relax myself to accommodate the second candle, I lost my grip on the first. It tilted. The candle dropped and the flaming wick gouged one of my husband's open eyes. Hot wax filled the socket. The flame guttered out, but the damage had been done, all because he wanted to watch.

He screamed and writhed on the bed, straining against his bonds. I scrambled off his chest and turned to look. The flame had gone out and for that much I felt thankful; I did not know what I would have done had the bed gone ablaze.

I kept Samuel tied up.

At first he cursed at me and whipped his head around like a defiant but fearful child. I straddled his midriff and bade him be still. He did his best. I used my fingernails to pluck out a piece of blackened wick that had pierced his eyeball. I boiled water and washed his eye. I carefully removed the wax that had dripped into it, and bandaged it. In the end, I had to cut the rawhide reins; he'd pulled them so tight when he struggled that I could not untie them with my fingers.

When I brought my husband our only bottle of whiskey, he struck me once, swatting me aside. Then he pried the cork out of the bottle and drank himself into oblivion.

I wept enough tears for both of us that night.

Samuel never regained his sight in that eye.

***

The sound of glass shattering from within our cabin startled me from my reverie. Had it been an empty whiskey bottle? Perhaps. My eyes stung with impending tears, as they always did whenever I dwelt upon the memory of that night. I heard the clatter of wood-on-wood, and visualized Samuel throwing his chair at the wall. I wondered if he felt as lonesome for me as I did for him. The front door slammed and I bounded around the side of the cabin but did not see my husband anywhere.

What a thrill to feel my heart pounding in my bosom! The gift bestowed by the Fortune Teller would be worth so much more than the coin I had given her. To be able to see Samuel, to touch him, and make love to him would be a blessing.

The katydids ceased their song. There came a rustle in the brush and Samuel appeared. I staggered back, knees wobbling like windblown stalks of wheat. We stood close enough that I could see his good pupil had dilated and his nostrils flared. I wondered if my scent, aroused as I was, overwhelmed him. My husband's mouth pulled back in a leer of recognition.

Even after the change, he knew me. And I knew him.

Fate can be cruel. The gypsy had worked her magic. Physical form would be mine every time the moon grew full. How could I have known I would find my husband in this state? Perhaps it is not so much fate, as it is a restoration of balance.

One aberration begets another.

Before I could blink, Samuel crouched and leaped through the air. His hackles were raised, his tail bristled. A ferocious snarl escaped his slavering jaws. Samuel's teeth glistened in the light of the full moon. My husband hit me in the chest with two huge paws and drove me into the dirt. Instinctively, I opened my legs. I grabbed fists full of his fur. He responded by nipping at my skin and lapping up the wet warmth that spurted from within me. He demanded much, but I felt willing to give it.

We were together again: rolling, pawing, thrusting, and gnawing. His brute strength overpowered me. With a thrill, I felt the muscles rippling beneath his fur. My bare feet kicked at the night sky as Samuel entered me. Never before had he felt so large. Like our first time together, my own blood facilitated his ingress. I needed to feel him, to join with him. The pain was tremendous.

The pain was exquisite.

The pain was... beginning to fade.

No! Why must it be over so soon? We could have–should have– had more time together!

Pain lanced through my flesh with each wet snap of tendons breaking against bloody fangs. I heard my own ribs cracking and realized the wolf-creature had moved past any suggestion of lovemaking. I wondered if my husband retained enough of his humanity in this state to feel the same sense of sorrow and loss that I did.

Numbed into shock, my limbs shook and I floated away from my body, just like when I had fallen from our wagon. I looked down at the man-wolf now devouring my heart. And why should he not? My heart belonged to him.

It paused. *He* paused.

Samuel threw back his head and unleashed a protracted, mournful howl.

I shared his sorrow but could not lend my voice to his cry.

A final vow came into my thoughts as I faded into nothingness: *I shall return to you, Samuel, and we will join together again.*

Every full moon. For love.

NO STRINGS
Josh Shiben

"I've got no strings," muttered Evan to himself through gritted teeth as he hauled his heavy body roughly up the side of the metal structure. The song had been stuck in his head, on repeat, for days, just endlessly looping like an annoying commercial tune. "To hold me up." Sweat of the exertion dripped from his body, making it sheen in the baking Virginia sun. He watched as his forearm gleamed in the light, watched it ripple and distort as something inside him slithered just beneath the surface. It was one of the worms, or parasites, or whatever they were. He wasn't sure. It didn't matter.

Evan grunted and continued climbing up the ladder. His mouth was so dry. So thirsty. They used to hurt, the worms. He remembered the pain they'd caused as they stretched his skin and bored through him. He remembered the fear, as he lay there on the hospital table, worrying that some parasite was turning him into a human-shaped block of Swiss cheese. But then, the doctor had given him drugs and it'd stopped. The pain. The crawling under his skin. They'd assumed the worms had died, but now Evan knew better. Poisons didn't kill them. Antibiotics just drove them deeper into his body. They were still there – still hiding inside of him. Burrowing into the very core of him. But when they came back, the pain stopped. Evan knew why – he was getting used to them. He was numb. Even the thought of pain was fuzzy – he knew it was an unpleasant sensation, but like a blind man thinking of color, he could not summon any impression of it. Pain, like most other sensations, was something that had passed out of his life. It had become an alien. He tried to worry about it, but all he felt was dry. Like a leaf in the fall, threatening to crumble to dust in the slightest breeze. He licked his lips and continued his climb.

"I've got no strings." He only knew the two lines, so he sang them over and over like a skipping record.

His hands were blistering on the rungs of the ladder, but he ignored them and climbed on. They didn't hurt, and he was too close to the top to stop now. It was so hard to climb with the heavy tools strapped to his back and his stomach distended the way it was; too heavy and awkward, and the writhing inside sometimes pushed him off balance. He had no attention to waste on something as trivial as blistering hands – he had to focus on gripping the ladder tightly, dragging himself up one rung at a time. Evan needed more water. He had to hurry.

He'd tried submerging himself in his bathtub, but it hadn't been enough. He'd just lay down there, watching as his breath bubbled to the surface, staring up through the ripples at the ceiling. He had drunk until he vomited the water back up, and then kept drinking, desperate for any kind of relief. After all of that, he'd still felt parched.

One summer, years ago, Evan had gone to the beach and gotten a nasty sunburn. But the burn hadn't hurt – it itched. The itch couldn't be scratched – it was under the skin, down deep in the muscle, and so, he had paced his room in agony, thinking that, if only he could cut the skin back, flay his chest and shoulders like a butchered animal, he might cure the irritation. That was his thirst now – a deep-seated, unquenchable itch, burning in his throat and mouth. It permeated every solitary cell in his body – his entire being cried out for water. He needed more than just a bathtub or a pool. He needed something drastic. He needed the impossible weight of thousands of gallons. He wanted to be buried in that crushing, impossible wetness – that black, freezing gulf, where even the sun cannot penetrate.

Evan had once seen a submarine flood in an old World War II movie he'd watched with his father. The hull had been breached by a depth charge, and the crew frantically sealed bulkheads to stop the implacably rising water from taking them all. As a child, Evan had stared at his ceiling, shuddering at the thought of being surrounded by the icy depths in that cold prison. He would lie awake, trying to exorcize fears of a black tide sliding up to consume him. Now, he fantasized about it. The icy cold grip of the water rising, promising more than he could ever drink.

He reached the catwalk, and with some effort, rolled himself onto the structure, where he rested only a moment before rising slowly to his feet. His legs were so weak and he was so heavy. He wondered how much of him was still Evan, and how much was worm? Two-thirds? Half?

He looked at his bloated, bulging stomach, wriggling with alien mass, and considered how much it must weigh. He'd been fit before all of this. Not in great shape, but good enough. He would have at least passed for a healthy person. Not now, though. The lesions on his flesh and undulating shapes under his skin removed any doubt as to his condition. He wanted to feel angry, or sad, or anything about it, but couldn't seem to muster the emotion. The thirst outweighed it all. He moved along the catwalk, to the small ladder leading to the top of the rounded tower, and with some effort, began hoisting himself up.

***

"No foreign travel or anything?" the doctor had asked. Sitting in his hospital gown, looking down at his feet glumly, Evan could only shake his head, "no." He'd never even left the state. He didn't have the money or the time away from work to go anywhere exotic. That was back when he still felt – the pain, the fear, the anger – it all bubbled up in him like a volcano. He was alive, then.

"Have you had any water that was maybe contaminated?" the doctor had tried. Again, he'd shaken his head. He only ever drank tap water – provided by the city, and purified by chlorine. The worms couldn't live in chlorine, could they? Tap water was clean.

***

Evan wet his lips again, and his tongue felt like sandpaper rubbing over a cracked and dried riverbed. With a grunt, he hoisted himself up another rung on the ladder. Some part of him realized he was dying, but he couldn't bring himself to be upset or bothered by the insight. The knowledge only gave him more motivation – better to receive this one last satisfaction than to die without it; a baptism to cleanse him, to wash away the wretchedness. It would bring relief. It had to.

"To hold me up," he whined out deliriously, his hands only two rungs below the edge of the structure. He looked down to see the tiny town beneath him, and briefly considered just letting go. The fall would certainly kill him – end this struggle in a splatter of worm-infested meat. But then, he'd never get his satisfaction – he'd die, never knowing relief. That thought alone was enough to spur him upward, toward the salvation only a few rungs above him. He tried to swallow, but his throat was too dry – his tongue felt like a burned piece of leather in his mouth, and he had to hold on tightly to keep from retching.

He pulled himself up the last two rungs and then clambered up on top of the hot metal structure. His arms and legs were weak with thirst, but with some effort, he hauled himself into the center of the circle. There was a round door in the roof, with a spinning handle on it that reminded him of the door of a vault. It was held in place by a simple padlock, and with a satisfying click of the bolt cutters he had brought along for just such a complication, Evan was through. His hands trembled with anticipation as he took the heavy crowbar he had carried up all this way and used it to force the wheel to slowly turn, unsealing the door with a metallic groan. He eased the door open, and was almost knocked backwards by the scent of chlorine that assaulted him.

When he'd first found out the worms were living inside of him, Evan had researched parasites. Now, as he looked down at the dark body of water, he remembered the Horsehair Worm. It reproduced in large, freshwater lakes, but grew inside the carapace of crickets. Sometimes, it would grow to be nearly a foot long, coiled tightly inside the little body like a spring. The problem was that, in order to complete its life-cycle, the worm had to return to the water. The solution was simple – it would convince its host to hurl itself into a lake; the vessel apathetic to its own self-destruction.

Evan remembered reading about the Horsehair Worm and wondering, how could something subvert an organism's drive for self-preservation so effectively? What did a cricket feel, when poised at the edge of the lake? He wondered, now, if it felt anything at all. Perhaps, only thirst. The thought almost stirred anger inside Evan's mind, but instead, he gazed down through the open portal and the feeling passed almost as quickly as it had started.

The water looked so calm and cool, and Evan was so thirsty. A soft drip from somewhere inside the water tower echoed through the door to Evan's ears, and without any more hesitation, he threw himself into the black water, mouth open and eager. His stomach ruptured when he entered the liquid and Evan felt the tightness in his gut relax, as thousands upon thousands of worms fled the confines of his body for the cool freedom of the water around him. They spilled out of him, like flies fleeing a rancid piece of road kill that'd been kicked, uncoiling from his belly like a disemboweled man's intestines.

The water tower echoed with the splashing of the worms as they undulated through the drinking water. Salvation choked Evan, pressing in on him from every direction. But he didn't thrash – he only opened his mouth as wide as he could. He'd finally found enough. He wasn't thirsty anymore. He'd never be thirsty again.

CLARISSA
Robert Essig & Jack Bantry

Clarissa cried. She cried a lot these days. Her life had been a wealth of tears and now she couldn't feel more helpless and desperate.

She rubbed her belly, bulging beneath a pair of swollen breasts that had become so tender that she wanted to scream into a pillow, but the pain in her breasts was nothing compared to the thoughts that constantly tormented her mind.

Clarissa had lost the urge to escape until recently. She was so tired, but she couldn't stay here and have her child subjected to the same abuse, the repeated rape. A sex toy trapped in a cellar. There was no way she could allow that monster to touch her child. Just the thought sent shudders through her slight frame. She didn't know the last time she had seen daylight. Had no idea how long she had been down there. She had nearly come full term and the length of the pregnancy was just a fraction of her imprisonment.

Clarissa couldn't remember her life before she was trapped in the cellar but she instinctively knew that she had never been a happy girl. The very idea of happiness must have come from some saccharine television sitcom she'd seen in a past that was further depressed in her mind with every dreary morning she woke up in captivity. Now, her mind was filled with dark corners and spider webs, dank, moldering odors mingling with her own sweat and bodily waste when her "bedpan" hadn't been properly disposed of.

Someone unlocked the basement door.

Clarissa wiped away the tears on her face, smearing through grime like cheap mascara.

The door opened. A man, cast in shadow, stood in the doorway. He was tall and heavy-set. She knew him as the Monster, any details hidden in the darkness.

She looked at him with large, sad eyes. They would have been beautiful had her life not been so tragic.

She rubbed her belly in a circular motion, a reminder that she was surviving for two. She had to get out of there so she could have this child and raise it on her own, away from the Monster.

If she couldn't escape, she wished the child dead, rather than lead a life like this.

The cellar was large but the furniture sparse. The Monster had, at some point, removed anything that could have been used as a weapon. Left her in darkness most of the time.

She had been waiting for the man to bring her food.

Clarissa clutched a hammer behind her back. She'd taken it from the Monster's toolbox when he'd put up a crudely handmade cot for the baby. So far, he hadn't noticed it missing.

She could feel the knot of worry twist her insides.

The baby kicked. That tiny foot reassured her of what she was putting at risk by attempting to escape. She rubbed her belly again with her free hand, soothing her nerves as much as possible. She would have one chance. If her aim was off, the consequences would be dire.

The man walked down the cellar stairs.

Clarissa gasped. Could she go through with it? What if she failed? He would punish her. He'd punish her anyway. That's what he normally did. He'd have rough, painful, degrading sex with her before returning upstairs, like nothing had happened, like she wasn't locked in his cellar.

He truly was a monster.

When he approached, he was looking around the cellar, probably admiring his handy work in constructing the cot. She hit him with the hammer and he collapsed like a cow in a slaughterhouse. She scurried up the stairs, towards the light shining down from the room above. Adrenaline surged through her veins. This was her chance. The Monster grabbed hold of her dress and yanked. The light above looked so far away and as she fell backwards, the light seemed to escape. It teased her, forever out of reach. Clarissa shook her head, tears running down her face, her mouth in a trembling rictus.

No!

The scream that erupted as she busted her tailbone on the concrete floor was agonized and shrill. She grabbed her belly, feeling something awful, something like she was going to be sick, only she wasn't going to vomit from her mouth, but from her vagina.

She'd dropped the hammer on the stairs as the Monster yanked her backwards.

He hefted her slack body into a standing position.

Clarissa screamed and flailed.

"Be quiet," he said. His voice was slurred like maybe he was dizzy from the hammer blow.

She felt utterly defeated, destined to be imprisoned in the dark cellar and abused, right up to her dying day.

What had she done to deserve such a fate?

His fist hit her in the belly, hard, the shock and pain enough to cause her to vomit. The man took a step back to avoid the bile spray, laughing at her as if she were some sideshow exhibit for his amusement.

"I said, be quiet. You'll wake your mother."

Clarissa's head rose, hair matted to her face with sweat and puke.

Mother?

Anger and hatred wracked her belly, then another. She looked up into the face of the man. The light from above showed her the image of her father. She clutched her abused belly, pain erupting from her womb, into her guts, threatening another bout of vomiting. That would have been a blessing, compared to what happened next.

Her body convulsed. Blood spread across the lower half of her filthy dress.

"I made that cot for nothing, now," he said.

Clarissa acted on impulse. Taking the man off guard, she darted up the stairs, towards the taunting light. She slipped and her already traumatized stomach lurched. The slip made her think of the blood running down the insides of her legs. She felt the man–was it really her father?–behind her. His fingernail scratched her calf when he tried to grab her. Instinctively, she kicked backwards and caught the man on the jaw. Looking back over her shoulder, she saw him clatter down the stairs. Relieved, Clarissa turned her body towards him. He lay unmoving. *Her father?* She was confused. Had she blocked it out all these years? Could her dad repeatedly rape her like this monster had? Hesitantly, she moved back down, towards the cellar floor, still no movement from the man. He didn't seem to be breathing. Had he broken his neck? She knelt down and looked him in the face.

It *was* her father.

And mother waited upstairs.

Clarissa turned away, and clutching her pained belly, walked back up the stairs. On her way, she picked up the hammer.

***

The light as she emerged into a house, she only vaguely remembered; seared into eyes that were only used to the dim glow of the solitary bulb hanging from the cellar ceiling. She blinked several times, trying to gain her focus, before proceeding and was startled by a gasp.

"Oh, it's...you," came an uneven voice that Clarissa hadn't heard in years. Her mother never had much of a soothing voice, not as far as Clarissa could remember.

Clarissa hefted the hammer above her head, eyes still adjusting. Through a gummy fog, she saw a sickly-thin woman standing in the kitchen. Couldn't make the features out. Clarissa blinked her eyes and things began to come into focus.

Has she been crying?

Emotion flooded through Clarissa. Her mother's face was sunken and sad, as if all the life had been sucked out of her with a vacuum. Her eyes looked too wide, in a head that appeared too large for the fragile frame of her body, hiding beneath a sundress like a dried up corpse beneath a shroud. Did her mother love her, had her father kept her down below against her mother's wishes? She yearned to be touched, embraced. She wanted her mother to make everything better.

Her mother's eyes darted down at the blood on Clarissa's legs. "Oh, my! You didn't hurt the baby, did you?"

Her mother completely disregarded the hammer and dashed across the linoleum floor, falling to Clarissa's feet, placing her hands over the protruding belly, as if praying to some absurd deity of the flesh.

The hammer wavered in Clarissa's hand. The feeling of this woman's hands on her belly drew attention to the fact that something was terribly wrong. One way, or the other, the baby was coming.

"Call an ambulance," said Clarissa, the words coming out in palsied syllables.

"No!" said her mother. "No ambulance, no police. No!"

"B-but..." Clarissa was confused.

"Get on the floor. I'll deliver the baby. Your father promised me another baby, you know. It's not yours. It's mine."

Clarissa's face wrinkled in disgust. Was the woman mad? It was *her* baby.

"No," said Clarissa. "I need an ambulance. Please, I need help."

Her mother stood up, the sad, forlorn look wiped away and replaced with one of contempt. She grabbed Clarissa by the arms and threw her to the ground. The impact sent a shockwave of pain through her womb and she knew the baby wouldn't survive. During the fall, the hammer leapt from her hand, hitting the linoleum floor with a dull thud.

With Clarissa's mother crouched over her, pinning her arms, Clarissa realized how weak she had become in the years of confinement. She had little muscle tone and was powerless to defend herself, even from a stick-and-bones, waste of a woman.

"Harold!" her mother called. "Harold, get up here and hold her legs! I want my baby!" Clarissa's mother erupted in tears. "You promised me a baby," she said through rising sobs.

Looking to the left and the right, Clarissa saw where the hammer had landed. Her mother let go of her arms and wrapped them around her belly, placing her ear to the bulge as if hoping to hear a sign of life.

Her mother swallowed hard and became frighteningly lucid. "If you're a boy, I'll name you George. If you're a girl, I'll name you Lilly. It'll be so nice to have a baby in the house again."

Clarissa grabbed the hammer, wrapping her fingers around the grip. When she lifted it, a scraping sound came from the weight of the hammerhead on the floor. Her mother's head popped up. Their eyes made contact as Clarissa swung the hammer. It made contact with her mother's temple. It wasn't much of a blow, but enough to startle the woman and cause her to fall to the side.

Clarissa maneuvered herself into a more compromising position. Pain radiated from her womb. It felt as if she was peeing all over herself, but she knew it was blood. She could feel herself getting weak from the loss of it.

Moaning, with a hand to her head, Clarissa's mother wavered as she attempted to get to her knees. Clarissa didn't allow this to happen. She'd hesitated before, the thought of killing her mother an abstraction that allowed for a disastrous hesitation, but now she realized that this was just a woman. *No, a monster*, just like her father. She smashed the hammer against her mother's head repeatedly before the blood on her hands caused the tool to slip and turn around. The final blow landed the claw end, where it stuck like an axe in a tree stump.

Clarissa screamed. Her eyes darted to the open cellar door and then to her mother's body and back to the door. She felt weak. The smell of blood was so heavy she could taste it. She scuttled out of the kitchen on her hands and knees, coughing and choking on the overwhelming, coppery odor in the room. She wasn't familiar with the house at all, but somewhere in the banished memories of a life lived before captivation, she remembered the numbers 911, emergency numbers to be dialed on the phone.

There was a phone on the littered coffee table in the living room. Clarissa dialed 911, said something unintelligible and then erupted in a fit of crying. The phone lay beside her, the tiny voice of the dispatcher calling for her. She was too weak. Couldn't move. A trail of blood followed her from the linoleum onto the carpeted floor. There was too much blood.

Too much.

She felt dizzy. Her eyes closed and opened again. The world seemed to spin, the red trail from the kitchen along with it.

The baby was dead.

PARADISE RAILROADED
Bernard McGhee

The miniature tree Simon was painting nearly slipped from his fingers when Dana walked into the guesthouse. Why was she there in the middle of the day? Simon looked up at her through his headband magnifier. She was out of focus, but Simon could tell she was wearing a black dress and hat and that's when he remembered it was Saturday and he was supposed to have been at her mother's funeral that morning.

Dana said nothing, but walked up to the end of the massive table that ran the length of the guesthouse and looked down at the model city. Simon put the tiny tree he'd been painting and the needle-thin paintbrush onto a towel on the edge of the table and took off the headband. Her eyes were red and her make-up smeared by wiped away tears.

"Her funeral was today," Dana said, her voice just loud enough to be heard above the clicks and whirrs of a model train that was weaving its way through the painstakingly crafted high-rises of the city's downtown area. "You were supposed to meet me at the church," she said. "But you've been busy with this again, I see."

Simon looked down. When he'd walked into the guesthouse the night before after Dana left to spend the night with her sister, he had only meant to spend a few minutes replacing the batteries on the motorized cranes at the shipping yard.

"Dana, I…." Nothing else came out. He could have said, "I'm sorry." But he had already said that so many times to her over the last few years. He could have said, "I was going to come, but I lost track of time." But she'd heard that before, too.

"I promise you, I really was going to be there," he finally said. "I was going to be there. It's just…" His voice trailed off again. Another train traveled along the edge of Dana's side of the table before disappearing into a tunnel carved into a hillside. It was too loud.

"Just…what?" Dana said, her eyes studying his face.

"I don't know," Simon said, looking away. "The park just looked so naked without any trees on it." He looked down at the floor and didn't lift his head until he heard her walk out of the guesthouse. He ran his hands through his thinning hair and took a step toward the door to go after her and stopped. What could he say?

He looked over the miniature city he'd built. When he started running out of space a year ago, he had most of the walls in the guesthouse knocked out, creating one large room. The model filled it up now and from under the table, wires snaked out across the floor in every direction. In Simon City, no one had to be on time for funerals. And if you had to get anywhere, a shiny, die-cast train was never more than forty-five seconds away. He looked at the tiny, plastic figurines; walking down sidewalks, playing soccer in the park, waiting on a train platform or examining a crate at the rail yard, and sighed.

He needed to talk to Dana. Running his hand along the control panel, he had just finished switching off all the trains, lights and other motorized cranes and amusement park rides in the city, when he spotted it. There was something written on the wall on the side of a bakery. "Graffiti?" he asked aloud. One by one, he had placed every building in the city, often attaching wires to small light bulbs inside, so the windows shined at night. There was no vandalism in his perfect city built along railroad tracks. He leaned in to look at the black letters scrawled across the plastic brick surface. "KERCHULGER HAS COME," it read.

When had Dana done this?

He slammed his first on the wall. "Jeez, be mad at me, but don't take it out on them," he muttered, as he rushed out of the guesthouse, across the backyard. He flung open the back door and stood in the kitchen. She wasn't in the room.

"Okay, I get it," he called out. "I know I screwed up. I'm sorry. But you didn't have to deface my model with that gibberish."

He waited for her to respond. Outside, a car door slammed shut and an engine started. He ran to the front door, but Dana was already driving down the street when he got outside. He called her cell phone but she didn't answer. He hung up when he heard her voicemail greeting. He stared at the empty space in the driveway where her car had just been. A knot formed in his stomach.

He went back inside. Upstairs, in their bedroom, several of her drawers had been pulled open and clothes taken out. The suit he was going to wear to the funeral was still hanging on the bathroom door. He tried calling her cell phone again. No answer. There was a lump in his throat. He fell onto the bed and closed his eyes. "Oh, God, why didn't I just set an alarm?" he said.

***

He drifted in and out of sleep for several hours before sitting up in bed. It was just after 2 a.m. Sunday morning. He tried calling Dana's cell phone again. Still no answer. He wandered through the house in a daze for a while and was walking out the back door to the guesthouse before he realized he'd decided to go there. It was stupid. The city that lived in the guesthouse was what caused all this – what caused most of his problems. But he needed to see it.

He opened the door to the guesthouse and stood still. Lights from hundreds of tiny windows filled the darkness. The room was alive with the sounds of trains moving along their tracks and cranes swiveling around. He took a step back from the doorway. "Who turned all this back on?" he whispered. Had Dana come back while he was asleep?

He walked in, his eyes scanning the railroad lines and then looked across the blocks of houses that gave way to office buildings and overpasses in the city's center. Even now, it was pretty to look at. He looked down at the hand-painted, plastic figurines that populated the city – all of them smiling as they stood frozen in time.

Three figurines, posed in an alley behind the library, caught his eye. He didn't remember putting anyone back there. He leaned in, taking care not to block the path of any trains or knock over a building. One man was standing behind another, holding his arms behind his back. In front of them, the third man had his fist raised, about to punch the man being held.

"Who did this?" Simon gasped as he pulled them apart. He laid the three figurines down on the edge of the table and looked around the rest of the city. No one was playing soccer on the playground anymore. Instead, a group of figurines, made up of adults and children, were crowded around a child who was on the ground, trying to rise up on his elbows and knees. Several in the crowd around the boy had their feet raised in a stomping motion. One man gripped a baseball bat with both hands as he held it above his head, about to bring it down.

Simon swept them up in his hands and threw them at the wall. "Who is doing this?" he cried. On the side of the post office next to the park, Simon saw more graffiti. He put on his headband magnifier and zoomed in on the writing. "BENEATH IT ALL, KERCHULGER WAITS," it read.

"Dana," he said. He pulled out his cell phone and called hers, again. She didn't pick up, but this time he stayed on when it went to voicemail. "Why are you doing this?" he pleaded. "Just, please come back home so we can talk."

He looked back over the city's stationary hustle and bustle for anything else out of place. After staring for several minutes, he stepped over to the control panel and turned it all off again.

***

He stayed out of the guesthouse for the rest of the day. Dana might have come home at any time and he didn't want her to see him there. In the afternoon, he tried calling her cell phone and still got no answer. He tried calling her sister, but got no answer there, either. By 9:30 p.m., he decided she probably wasn't going to come back today. Simon had to go back to work the next morning, but before he went to bed, he gave in and allowed himself to have one more, quick look.

***

As he walked up to the guesthouse, he could hear the sounds of tiny motors running inside. He stood still in the backyard for a moment, before walking up to the door and opened it with a sweaty hand.

Everything was on again and the figurines had been moved around. He walked up to the table and, for several minutes, could only stare at how Simon City's plastic residents were posed.

In the amusement park, a riot had broken out. A crowd of figurines were punching, kicking, biting and clawing at each other, as a miniature Ferris wheel merrily made its rotations. Downtown, a row of six, headless figurines, were lined up side-by-side on a sidewalk. In the street in front of them, a smiling woman in a dress stood with her arms raised. In one hand, she held a large knife. In the other hand, she held a man's plastic, severed head by the hair. In the shipping yard, a woman was hanging upside-down from a streetlight by a rope tied around her ankles. A crowd of people, gathered around her, appeared to be pummeling her with sticks, fists and feet. At the school playground, a model train clicked down a nearby track while rows of children knelt with their hands tied behind their backs and men holding large knives stood guard around them.

And graffiti was scrawled in black and red letters on walls all around the city. "KERCHULGER LOVES US ALL," proclaimed the wall on the side of a house. "MY LIFE FOR KERCHULGER," read the side of a container on the edge of the shipping yard. "YOUR PAIN BELONGS TO KERCHULGER," read the wall of a downtown alley.

Simon closed his eyes and took a step back from the table. He took another step and his back hit the wall.

He opened his eyes. The woman who had been holding the knife and the head was standing with her arms at her side, now. She still had the knife, but the head was gone. Simon screamed and wrenched the power cord that went to the control panel from the wall socket. The city went silent and dark and Simon ran out of the guesthouse, slamming the door shut behind him.

***

He couldn't sleep that night. The next day, he could barely stay awake as he sat at his desk in the IRS processing center, as screen after screen of tax records fluttered in front of his glazed eyes. The columns of numbers all looked like railroad tracks and he wondered if he'd ever get to talk to Dana again.

***

He paused when he stepped back into the house after work and listened for Dana. There was only silence. Simon sat at the kitchen table and looked out at the backyard. He trembled, then stood and closed the curtains.

He tried watching TV, but couldn't find any shows about trains. He called Dana's cell phone again. No answer. He looked out the window again, at the guesthouse. He started shaking again, but clenched his fist.

"I built it. I've got to take it back," he whispered. And then louder: "I've got to take my city back."

***

The sun was going down as Simon trudged toward the guesthouse. He stopped when he reached the door and listened.

He didn't hear anything coming from inside. He took a deep breath and opened the door.

Inside, the room was dark, except for a single light in the center of the model city. The trains sat motionless on their tracks and none of the cranes or carnival rides or drawbridges were moving. Simon walked along the side of the table. The dim light showed empty streets and yards.

The light was coming from City Hall in the center of the city. In front of it, a crowd of plastic figurines were gathered in a semi-circle. They were all on their knees, arms raised in worship. Something inside City Hall was making soft, scratching sounds. A shadow danced across the crowd posed outside, as it moved in front of the light bulb inside the building.

Simon looked around the rest of the city. There were no figurines anyplace else but at City Hall. "There should be more of them here," he whispered. "Where are the rest of them?"

There was a click as the entire room was bathed in light from the ceiling. Simon jumped back from the table. Dana was standing by the door with her hand on the light switch.

"Jesus, I didn't even hear you come in," he said, holding his hand over his heart.

Dana stared at him.

Simon took a moment to catch his breath and then said, "I'm really glad you came back. I've been wanting to talk to you, so badly."

"I know," Dana said. "I saw your calls. But I needed some time away from you to think, Simon. About us. About everything." Her lip quivered and tears filled her eyes. "You really let me down, Saturday. I needed you and you weren't there."

"I know," Simon said. "I'm so sorry. I wish to God I could go back to that morning. I know I hurt you. But please, I beg you…"

"I love you, Simon," she said, interrupting him. "I do. But things can't keep going on like this." She looked at his model city. "I don't understand why playing with your trains has such a hold on you. I don't. But, I realized I'd rather have you, with your train set, than not at all." She looked back at him. "But, I need to know I actually *have* you, Simon. I *need* to know that you're really in this, too."

"You do," Simon said. "And I *am* in this with you."

He walked toward her, his arms outstretched to embrace her. One of the trains whirred to life and began moving down its track. Out of habit, Simon's eyes scanned along the rest of the track as the train clicked along and he saw a plastic, young girl, laid across the track. Several men, holding sticks and knives, were standing around the track. Next to the track, a man and a woman had their wrists tied above their heads, to the branch of a tree. The man and woman at the tree were both looking at the girl on the tracks, their faces contorted into silent screams as they pulled against the ropes.

"Holy shit," Simon said. The train was just an inch away from the girl when he swatted it off the track. The train tumbled through a cluster of trees, knocking them down, before resting on its side on a street leading into a neighborhood of small houses.

"See what they've been doing?!" he said, not realizing he was yelling. "I can't take my eyes off them for even a second, now!"

He turned back to Dana but lost his voice as anger filled her bloodshot eyes.

She took a step back.

"Dana, wait please…"

"No," she said, her voice hoarse. "I'm not spending another *second* of my life waiting for you. Have fun with your trains."

She ran out of the guesthouse.

"Wait, I'm sorry. Please don't leave," Simon said as he followed her out.

"Don't *touch* me. Don't come *near* me," Dana snarled, rushing across the backyard.

"Just give me a chance to talk," Simon pleaded. She was almost to the side of the house and Simon put his hand on her arm to slow her down.

"I said don't *touch* me!" Dana yelled, as she turned and threw a wild punch that caught Simon in the jaw. "Oww. Shit!" she cried and cradled the hand that had punched him in her other hand.

She turned around again and went around the house to the driveway. Simon stood there as she walked, out of sight, to the front of the house and touched his jaw. A few seconds later, a car engine started and Dana pulled out, screeching tires on the pavement as she drove off.

Simon's vision blurred and a tear ran down his cheek. He went into the house and collapsed onto the sofa. He spent the next three hours staring at the ceiling and thinking of Dana. He told himself he'd take the model apart and throw the trains away, just before falling asleep.

***

He was standing when he woke up. The bare wall he was facing wasn't the wall in the den. His neck and body were stiff. He groaned and clenched his teeth as he turned to look around the room. He almost jumped when he saw two people standing in a doorway, leading outside, but his stiff body only shuddered. Looking again, Simon realized they were two, life-sized, plastic statues of smiling police officers. Both had one hand up in a friendly wave.

Next to them, a glass-less window looked out to an empty, dimly-lit street. Simon strained to turn his head and look at the rest of the room. There was no furniture and the off-white walls were bare. He looked down at the floor and saw that his body was made of hard plastic.

Breathing quickly and struggling against the plastic that coated him, he brought his hands up in front of his face and stared at his palms.

"What is this?" he asked, as he slowly, painfully, closed his hands and opened them again. His mouth could barely make the words. All he saw was plastic. "What is this? What's happening to me?"

He put a hand to his face, but felt nothing.

"What's happening to me?!" he yelled to the plastic statues. "What's happening to me?!"

He fell to his knees with a thunk, and plastic hands clacked against his plastic face as he covered his eyes and screamed.

Out of breath, he took his hands away from his face. It was easier to move now. He looked at his hands again. Color was bleeding into the off-white plastic. Lines and wrinkles rose out of what had been a smooth surface. After a few moments, Simon saw skin and fingernails again. He put his hand to his face, again, and smiled as he felt his fingers move across his cheek.

"There he is," a voice said. Startled, Simon looked up. Two police officers, which were identical twins, were walking to him. The two statues were gone. "You need to come with us, Sir," one of the officers said, as they helped Simon to his feet.

"What's going on?" Simon asked. "Where are we going?"

"The master has called for you," the officer said.

"I don't understand," Simon said, as they led him out of the house and down the sidewalk. "Who are you talking about and where am I?"

"You don't know where you are?" one of the officers asked with raised eyebrows.

"Show some respect," the other officer said. "He's the creator." Then he said to Simon, "You're in Simon City, Sir."

Simon could only stare back at him for a moment, as they walked.

"Simon City?" he asked. "As in, *my* Simon City? My model train set?"

"Not sure what you're talking about, Sir," the officer said. "But, we're all real, here. You helped make us that way."

"Hold on a second, what about what I saw before?" Simon asked. "Why was there all that killing and violence?"

"We had to take care of the non-believers," the officer said. "The ones who wouldn't accept him."

"Him, who? Who are you talking about?"

"Kerchulger, of course," the officer said. "He gave us a purpose. He made this all mean something. Our lives, our joy, our pain, it all belongs to Kerchulger."

They reached a large square. Across the square, sat City Hall. A light from inside the hall shined out through the windows and illuminated the square. Beyond City Hall, the darkened high-rises of downtown Simon City were barely visible.

A crowd of people were gathered in front of the hall. It all looked so different from the town Simon had spent months and months piecing together. He had never seen it at eye-level before.

The crowd silently parted as the officers led Simon through. Most of the people in the crowd looked down as he walked by. A few nodded at him. At the front of the crowd, a man in a white robe stood on the steps leading to the front door of City Hall. His robe was covered in dried blood.

"The master willed it and so it has come to pass," the man in the robe said to the crowd. "The creator has come. All praise goes to Kerchulger."

"All praise to Kerchulger," the crowd responded in unison.

"What is all this?" Simon asked, trying not to look at the bloodstains on the man's robe. "Why am I here?"

"Because, you are the creator. We owe our existence to you," the man said. "But the master can't keep tolerating your blasphemies."

"Blasphemies? I don't even know what you're talking about," Simon protested.

"You interfered as we tried to chastise those who wouldn't believe," the man said. "You disrupted the sacrifice, even going so far as to derail one of the sacred trains."

"Wait a second," Simon said. "Are you talking about the girl on the track? Is that what that was? What was I supposed to do? She was about to get killed."

"Her death belonged to Kerchulger!" the man yelled.

Behind Simon, angry murmurs rippled through the crowd and it felt like the people were creeping closer to him. He thought of the headless bodies lined up on the sidewalk.

The man in the robe opened his mouth, as if he was about to say something else, then looked to the doors behind him.

"Yes, please. Tell me what you would have us do," the man said as he turned and walked to the closed front doors of City Hall. He put his ear to the building's double-doors and waited.

Inside City Hall, something stirred – something *big*. Behind him, the crowd became hushed and when Simon glanced over his shoulder, they were all on their knees. He looked back at the building. Something moved past the windows. Simon only got fleeting glimpses, but it was huge and moved with heavy steps on several, black, spindly legs.

At the doors, the man in the white robe cupped his ears and squinted his eyes as he listened. Simon tried to listen too, but all he could hear was a faint buzzing. The man's eyes widened and he smiled as he turned back to the crowd.

"Give praise, for Kerchulger is most merciful," he announced. "Because you are the creator, the master will allow you to make amends for the sacrifice you've stolen from him. Kerchulger be praised!"

"All praise to Kerchulger!" the crowd responded.

"Bring him to the tracks," the man instructed.

The two officers handcuffed Simon's hands behind his back as the crowd closed around them.

"Wait, let me go," Simon said. "What's happening? Why do you all keep calling me, 'the creator'? I didn't create any of this. I just built a train set."

"But, you did create this," the man in the robe said, as he walked down the steps to him. "The master told me about you. This place was built by all your missed moments. The life you neglected now flows through us. But it was Kerchulger who gave us purpose, and through him, your life, too, will now have a purpose."

Each one gripping Simon's arms, the two officers took him from the square. The man in the robe walked next to them and the crowd followed, as the officers took Simon through a cluster of trees. They crossed a grassy field and stopped next to a set of train tracks. Simon looked at some trees lying on their side nearby and swallowed.

"Despite your efforts to thwart him, we were able to repair the train and return it to the tracks," the man said. "And now, Kerchulger will have what is his."

The officers pushed Simon forward and made him sit down on the iron railroad track, his legs stretched out across. With a second set of handcuffs, the officers chained his feet by the ankles, to the center of one of the wooden planks that ran between the rails and made him lay on his back, with his thighs resting on the track. Simon realized what they meant to do.

"No, wait!" he yelled. "Please. I'm sorry about before. I didn't know what was going on."

Simon's hands were still cuffed behind his back and the officers held him down by his shoulders. Under his legs, the track began vibrating as a train rumbled towards them.

"Please, don't do this," Simon begged. "I'll do anything. I'll build more. I'll put up whatever you want."

The officers only stared down at him with blank expressions. The tracks' vibrations were getting stronger. The train was speeding toward them, clanging and hissing, as it lumbered along the rails.

"Please, just give me another chance!" Simon shouted, as he struggled against the officers holding him in place. But he could barely hear his own words. The man in the robe leaned into view. He was kneeling on the ground next to them and put a hand to Simon's cheek.

"It's okay. You don't have to be afraid, I promise," he said, staring into Simon's eyes. "Your pain will belong to Kerchulger."

Simon stopped struggling, took a slow breath and gazed up at the starless night sky.

The train roared by, spreading a red surge of pain through Simon's legs. His throat suddenly felt gravelly and sore, as he looked up at the thunderous, sparking blur of metal that was grinding his legs to pulp. And then it was gone, leaving Simon's ears filled with a strange sound that he realized, a heartbeat later, was his own screaming.

The officers pulled him up and uncuffed his hands. Still screaming, and in a haze of agony, Simon barely noticed. He couldn't take his eyes off the bleeding, ragged stumps that used to be his legs.

"Hurry, and get him into position, before the train comes back around," the man in the robe told the officers. "He still has more to offer up."

Behind them, someone in the crowd yelled, "Kerchulger loves us all!" and others hummed in response.

The officers turned Simon over onto his front, stretched his arms out onto the gore-smeared tracks and cuffed his wrists.

"This isn't right," Simon said, sobbing. "I didn't build it for this. This was supposed to be a happy place."

The man in the robe shrugged. "When did this place ever bring you happiness?"

The tracks were vibrating again. Simon took one, last look at his arms, as the sound of the train grew louder in the distance, and thought of Dana.

***

"You know, he probably just ran off with another woman," Detective Freedy said, as he looked over the silent expanse of the model city.

"His wife said he didn't have a life outside working on his train set," Detective Conner said. "If he wasn't at his job, he was in here. Doesn't seem like the kind of routine that lends itself to meeting other women."

"Well, wherever he is, I've got to hand it to him," Freedy said. "This takes a lot of talent."

"No, this takes a lot of obsession," Conner said. "From what she told us, sounds like this was the reason she was getting ready to divorce him. That's a talent I don't think I…Wait. Looks like we've got some dried blood over here."

"Where?" Freedy asked, as his eyes ran back and forth across the town.

"Right here, on the tracks here."

"Looks like just a couple drops. He could have done that by accidentally cutting himself."

"Maybe," Conner said. "But take a picture of it, just in case."

"God, I hate missing person cases," Freedy said, as he walked around to the other side of the table, camera in hand.

"Look at all this," Conner said, shaking his head. "He even put in little, plastic people, to live here. This guy had way too much time on his hands." He leaned in for a closer look.

"What do you see?" Freedy asked.

"Looks like one of the plastic figures here is just a headless torso, impaled on a pole," Conner said. "Right here, in front of what I guess is City Hall."

"Yeesh," Freedy said. "Well, she did say she thought he was losing it. Want me to take a picture of it?"

"Sure, but it's just more evidence that this guy's a weirdo, which we already know," Conner said. "Come on. Let's take one last look through the house and then head back to the station and see if we can get his bank and phone records."

Conner took a few steps toward to the door to the guesthouse and then looked back at Freedy, who was still standing at the table after taking another picture. "Something wrong?"

"No," Freedy said, after a moment. "I thought I heard something moving around in the model somewhere, for a second. Maybe I'm losing it, too." He paused.

"Yeah, let's head out. Wherever he is, he's obviously not here."

BUY...PSYCHE...KILL
Ken Goldman

(1) BUY...

"Every time you miss your childhood, ride on a bicycle."
– Mehmet Murat Ildan, Turkish Playwright

At 6:17 p.m. on Monday, April 21, 2014, fifty-year-old, Arthur Fitz, died a little.

At first, it seemed hardly a dramatic event; a slight grimace, followed by a clutch at his chest over his wife's second serving of mashed potatoes. Dora noticed her husband's face had gone ashen and that his lips formed soundless words, like some drooling, old fart, whose dentures had loosened.

"Arthur, are you feeling all right?"

What he muttered wasn't much help. "I...I'm..."

Fitz was feeling very far from all right. Mashed potatoes dripping down his chin, fingers splayed; he clutched his chest harder while his mind went into free fall.

So, this is how it happens, death. The insidious bastard decides it's your time to punch out, sneaks up on you while you're having your dinner, and just like that...?

"Call 911..." Fitz managed. Dora, unusually level headed, already was pressing the numbers into her phone. But her trembling voice revealed she recognized serious trouble when she saw it. "Emergency," became the last word Arthur Fitz heard from her before his lights went out, but one thought remained clear.

Insidious bastard...

***

"If you must cheat, cheat death."
– Unknown

Luckily, Mr. Death was just passing through; his brief visit, a false alarm. It must have been morning, early enough for dappled sunlight to shine into Arthur Fitz's hospital window, bathing him in life-affirming brilliance. Or maybe the sun was setting. He didn't care. He was alive.

"Ummmghhh..." he mumbled, re-entering the world of the living. He hadn't crossed over, nor seen any white light, except for the sun, although, a familiar angel stood alongside his bed. Dora brushed some wispy hair from her husband's forehead.

"Good morning, and welcome back. You didn't have to go to all this trouble if you didn't like my cooking."

Fitz noticed the network of wires taped to his chest, leading to some video game-like apparatus. The monitor of an electrocardiogram showed the dancing blips of his heartbeats. Dora forced a smile.

"Your ticker has been playing Pong all morning. The cub scout doctor here says your heart is finally behaving, so there won't be any, 'I-see-dead-people,' surprises here."

"Dora, I thought I'd bought it. Where am I?"

"Exotic Shore Memorial, my love. You had a 'heart episode,' a little fibrillation, no actual attack. A kind of 'elaborate muscle spasm,' Doc said, but serious enough. The man looked like he just started shaving last week, but he seemed pretty confident you're okay, now." Dora squeezed her husband's hand. "A man your age is staring down the barrel of a loaded gun. This was my fault, too. You fell into a second helping of mashed potatoes that *I* put on your plate."

It was just like Dora to feel responsible. The woman doted on him far beyond her wifely requirements. Fitz admitted changes had to be made. His heart episode, or whatever his doctor called it, *(muscle spasm, my ass!)* had all the symptoms of the real deal. As with his bouts with acid reflux and his (often futile) attempts to pee past an enlarged prostate, Arthur knew his middle years were fucking with him, big time.

"You've had your wake up call, my darling, and you're going on a diet the minute I get you home, so kiss those boardwalk pizzas goodbye. I don't plan on collecting your insurance, just yet. You *have* been paying those premiums, right?"

With his feeding tube still inserted into his wrist, Arthur pinched his wife's ass. The woman's smile seemed damned good medicine. "Sorry, honey. I'm leaving it all to my mistress. She gets the shore house and all the rest. You and Julie get nothing. But, I really did enjoy these twenty-five years."

Dora's smile twitched a little. She squeezed his hand harder. "I'm glad our daughter married well, then. As for me, that ass you just pinched still has plenty of mileage. I mean, just in case I need to put it to good use."

A skinny nurse appeared at the door, a woman whose age seemed impossible to determine. If she were forty, she looked great – in her twenties, not so much. She partially closed the blinds. "Too much sun beating down on you, in your condition, isn't good. I see you're back with us, Mr. Fitz. We have a few things to discuss." Whipping out a thermometer, she stuck it in her patient's mouth. "This'll keep you quiet, while I talk. You had quite a scare last night, didn't you? You *do* want to see old age? I'm not talking just salads and wheat germ, mister." She inspected the thermometer, seemingly satisfied.

A crappy diet of vegetables and high fiber with no carbs –

essentially the elimination of anything tasting good – Arthur had expected that lecture from Nurse Rianne, as her nametag, indicated. Maybe he could live with that, at least, some of the time. But, there was more.

"My husband doesn't exercise, Nurse. He just turned the big five-oh, and I can hear the man's bones creak when he climbs out of bed." Arthur shot Dora a dirty look. She shot another right back. "Go ahead and hate me, lover, but I want you around for your old farthood."

"I think that's already underway."

Nurse Rianne managed a smile. "Then you may want to familiarize yourself with a treadmill or an exercise bike, Mr. Fitz, some daily routine at the local spa or at home. I'm not suggesting a decathlon, just something to get you off your ass, if you'll permit me to be blunt. That spare tire you're carrying isn't doing you any good, and it's probably what sent you here. A man your age..."

Fitz hated any sentence containing those words, and his attention ended there. Trotting on some treadmill meant an hour staring at the fat ass of whoever worked the machine in front of his, and an exercise bike seemed a tiring trip to nowhere. But he smiled at the scrawny nurse and feigned agreement, like some Bobblehead doll, hoping his doing so would get him out of this bed by noon.

"Yes, I think I can do that."

"Are you a Star Wars fan, Mr. Fitz?"

Arthur had no idea where Nurse Rianne was going with that. "I've seen it."

The woman scribbled her initials on her patient's release form.

"Then, don't think. *Do.*"

***

Arthur Fitz *did*.

No treadmill could entice him to exercise, no stationary bike, either. But, a real bike – a *bicycle*, like that memorable

3-speed model he had as a kid (*no, he could afford better than that now!*)…Oh, hell yes! A smart looking bike would give him incentive to pedal his way back to good health and get the old ticker doing the Boogie Woogie in no time. Add to that the advantage of watching all those young girls of summer who strolled the boardwalk. But no wussie, single-speed bicycle would do, nuh uh. Heart episode aside, Arthur Fitz was still a man, and that called for a man's racer, worthy of that one-balled, steroid factory, Lance Armstrong.

He found the place, called *Spokespeople,* online – a clever name for a boardwalk bike shop. With an array of road bikes, mountain bikes, touring cycles and racers, the place seemed just what the doctor (or bony-assed, Nurse Rianne) ordered. A sleek, black English Racer caught his attention.

"She's a beauty, all right," the pimpled sales kid told him. "Twenty-one speed Shimano gearshift, aluminum frame and rim wheels, compact and light enough to carry on your back. Well, that's just shoptalk. What kind of biking are you into? Road? Mountain? Pleasure or commute? Speed or comfort?"

"Look at me, kid. Does this body suggest the Tour De France? I haven't biked in years, and a tough hill might send my ticker back to the shop. You don't think this bike is a little more muscle than I need for the Boardwalk World Cup?"

"This cycle isn't quite a Harley, but twenty-one speeds will take you where you want to go. That's what's important, right?"

"The price tag is $1,221, and that's damned important, too. My wife may kill me before any hills do." Fitz thought that one over. This bike would show that he took his exercise routine seriously. "Oh, screw it. I'll take it." He noticed a sharp-looking, protective bike helmet on the rack, black with yellow lightning bolts on each side. "I'll take that, too. Reminds me of The Flash." The kid clearly had no idea who that superhero was.

"You want the full biking gear package: shorts and jersey to go with the helmet? Day-Glo is good for nighttime rides."

Fitz managed not to laugh. "No, I think I'll pass on the complete asshole look, for now."

The kid pulled the head gear from its rack. "Well, you'll enjoy this helmet, 'cause it's got a radio built right in. You just smack the side here and, *presto!* – Full digital stereo, enough to keep the world out of your head, 'cept for Aerosmith or Led Zep, or whatever you like listening to. Newest thing for the boardwalk biking crowd."

Kid, you wouldn't know Aerosmith if you woke up with Steven Tyler spooning your ass.

"Sold," Fitz said. The sales kid put batteries into the helmet and Fitz tried it on, tapping the power button on the side. On FM 101 *(WJRZ in Jer-sey, playin' the oldies for you, day and night!),* Blondie's Debbie Harry was bitching about her heart of glass.

It seemed appropriate.

(2) PSYCHE...

"If you could read my mind, love,
What a tale my thoughts could tell..."
　　　　　　　　　–Gordon Lightfoot

Fitz rode the new racer home, routing his trip along the boardwalk's eight-mile stretch, although, the morning hours for Atlantic City cycling had passed. During the summer months, the city's cops came down hard on the kids for that *(no mowing down of the cash-paying casino customers, please)*, but the tourist season hadn't started and a local official probably would let him off with a warning. He was wobbly with his balance, but the bike provided a smooth ride. Pedaling felt practically effortless *(twenty-one gears!)* and gear #6 seemed about right for the boards. Fitz wondered if biking like this counted as exercise, at all. It certainly brought back childhood memories – those moments of breathing in fresh air while enjoying every breath – returning him to a time when a boy could be alone with his thoughts.

Fitz tuned into FM 101, where Céline Dion's lyrics vanquished the sounds of the boardwalk strollers. Along with the occasional nights he felt his oats with Dora, this was exercise he could live with, and as Céline insisted through the speakers, the heart does go on. His own ticker certainly proved that. Deciding to challenge himself, Fitz snapped the handlebar shifter to gear #7.

WATCH IT, MISTER!

Distracted, Fitz almost hit some kid navigating a skateboard, going the opposite direction. Céline fell silent, and somehow, the kid's words came through, unimpeded. Fitz squeezed the hand brakes and turned, to see the boy flat on his ass. He couldn't have been more than fourteen. Fitz walked the bike towards him, prepared to offer an apology.

You old shit! Why don't you look where you're going?

Fitz removed the helmet. "Are you okay? Do you need some help? I was distracted, and I'm really sorry." His parental instinct kicked in. "It's none of my business, but do you talk to your mother with that mouth?"

The kid just looked at him. Getting to his feet, he rested one foot on his board, expertly snapping it into his hands. "Mister, I didn't say anything."

"I'm not an old shit, thank you. I'm an accountant! I went to Princeton!" Fitz realized he sounded exactly like what the kid had called him. He put the helmet back on, adjusted its strap. "Well, like I said, I'm sorry. And watch the language." He got moving.

You're fucking crazy, Mister. You know that?

Fitz turned, looked at the kid again. He heard words, but the kid's mouth wasn't open. Maybe his perceptions were clouded because of the meds the Cub Scout doctor had prescribed? The damned Beta blockers, whatever they were. The sun beating down on his head probably didn't help, either. The kid's curses died out as Skater Boy disappeared down the boardwalk.

Damned punk. Fitz recalled some old lady who used to chase him and his pals off her lawn. Those times seemed a hundred years ago, and now, here he was, coming off like some old geezer, lecturing a fourteen-year-old about boardwalk etiquette.

Snapping the gearshift to #9, he tapped the helmet again. "Heart and Soul," by The Cleftones, came on. He knew the song well, smiling at its ability to bring him back to simpler times. In seventh grade, he had gotten one memorable erection, dancing to that song with Nancy Snyder, whose huge jugs reminded him of Annette Funicello.

'Hard-on and soul, I fell in love with you...'

Yes Nancy, that's my stiffy grinding into you, all right...

At his 25th reunion, Nancy Snyder no longer looked like Annette Funicello. The real Annette was already dead, and wasn't that a nice thought to have on this beautiful spring day?

9th gear proved taxing and Fitz returned to 7th. Interrupting the Cleftones, something came through the speakers.

...should ask him to move off the boards...

A beefy cop stood by the railing along the promenade's ocean side, near a sign: NO BICYCLES ALLOWED AFTER 10 A.M. The cop stared at him.

Fitz stopped. "Heading home, officer. Sorry!" The officer's expression remained fixed.

He's not some wise-ass kid. No point making a stink before the season even starts. Tell him to have a nice day and keep moving...

Then, "Hey, bud, it's okay! Boardwalk's not too crowded, like summer. Just move along. You have a nice day!"

Fitz got moving again, but his brain raced. It wasn't the meds screwing with his head. The helmet, this bike in 7th gear, somehow working together...

On 101, Janis Joplin begged some guy, in bluesy fashion, *"TAKE ANOTHER LITTLE PIECE OF MY HEART NOW, BABY!"*

Today, Oldies 101 seemed obsessed with one common theme.

Arthur Fitz's heart pounded as he pedaled faster.

***

This is nuts...

Somehow, the mind adapts to insane circumstances; this was Fitz's rumination, while speeding past clusters of boardwalk strollers. As clearly as this thought occurred, he heard stranger's thoughts with similar clarity. It felt uncomfortable, his invasion of others' privacy, but how could they know he had tuned into snippets of their innermost secrets?

I won't pay for her lunch. Why did I agree to meet this pig?

...birthday coming soon. Don't want a damned party – why can't you understand that?

Eat your way down this boardwalk 'til you fucking bust, you fat cow...

...cheap tramp. Probably a hooker...

It was like channel surfing, picking up meaningless dribbles of conversation, muffled enough so that there seemed little difference among the riot of voices layered on top of more voices. The thoughts were distinctly male, and matching the cacophony of words with the guy thinking them seemed impossible. Maybe that was a good thing.

Yeah, I'd do that one...no, not her...maybe the blonde...

What more does the bitch want from me?

... old, getting ugly. So beautiful, once. Damn...

Maybe I should kill her.

Bonnie Tyler interrupted the racket, in full digital stereo.

"Nothin' I can do, a total eclipse of the heart..."

Fitz slammed his palm against the helmet. The singer fell silent, but not the voices.

Look at those tits.

...if I could get her in bed I'd...

How am I supposed to pay for...?

I should kill her, the lying cunt. Kill her today.

Fitz squeezed the hand brake.

What was that last one...?

His rear wheel skidded, but he managed to stop without tumbling off the bike. He studied the men walking alone, then those with women or in small groups. The racer inert, his helmet's speakers fell silent. It mattered little that Fitz had inadvertently violated the laws of nature; that he had effortlessly tuned into some sort of, *Outer Limits*, as if it were the local radio station. Having recently gone one-on-one with Death, accepting the impossible seemed less difficult than it would have a week earlier. Fitz felt more bothered by what he had heard from...

...from someone nearby!

Kill her. Hop on my bike and kill her...

(3) KILL

"The dumber people think you are, the most surprised they're going to be when you kill them."
—William Clayton

...Kill her?

Fitz thought that over.

Nah! Nuh uh!

Probably some pissed off jerk, excising some demons, whose woman had driven him momentarily crazy. But just to be sure...

Circling again, Fitz studied faces, but expressions revealed little. A few strollers stared belligerently back, as if he had invaded some personal space. He returned a dumb-ass grin and kept pedaling. Spotting a teen walking with his hand gripped inside his girl's ass pocket, he crossed him off the list. That horny kid's thoughts were on that shapely young ass. Fitz didn't need to read the kid's mind to know that.

He set a bead on another couple, probably married. Maybe in their forties, they weren't talking to each other. *(Nothing new there!)* The guy wore earbuds; probably, he was listening to the Phils lose another one to the Cubs. Not him, either. Studying more faces, Fitz repeated his revolutions.

…Bash her fucking brains out, cut her stinking throat!

A muscle-shirted guy, maybe early thirties, stood away from the strollers. Alone, by the railing, watching the surf, he seemed the type who probably rode a bike, as he had revealed, all right…no fucking Schwinn, but some gutsy road demon, like a Harley. An over-sized tattoo on his arm showed a serrated knife dripping blood. *(Well, of course!)* The stranger turned, his eyes following Fitz as his bike made another pass. The man was good-looking, but not the guy you would want to meet in a dark alley. Averting his stare, Fitz felt his face go flush. He kept a respectable distance from his subject as another thought came through the speakers.

Thinks she can just fuck me and forget me? She needs to die. And what's this putz on the bicycle looking at?

Fitz couldn't exactly ride up to tap the brute on his tattooed bicep and ask him to rethink his blood lust over coffee at Starbucks. He couldn't keep staring at him, either, if he wanted to keep his teeth.

The young man reached into his pocket. Was he hiding a gun there, or maybe a knife, like his tattoo displayed? He could have just been scratching his balls. Dagger Man was on the move, now. The boardwalk crowd had thickened, and the stranger could easily disappear into it. Fitz waited until the guy walked a safe distance, adjusted his helmet, and then pedaled. He had no idea what he was going to do, or what he *could* do.

"Hey! You! Stop your bike!" an unsmiling cop shouted at Fitz. Having no choice, Fitz squeezed his hand brake. The cop approached him.

"Officer, I'm in a bit of a hur–"

"You know you're not supposed to be riding on the boardwalk past ten? Dismount the bike, please." The young cop's timing couldn't have been worse.

"I'll get off the boardwalk, officer. I'm heading off, now. I just need to–" Fitz craned his neck, tried to spot the guy he was following. The cop didn't seem happy with his preoccupation.

"Off the bike and remove the helmet. Now!" He pointed to the NO BICYCLES ALLOWED AFTER 10 A.M. sign on the railing behind him. Those warnings seemed to be everywhere. "What you're going to do is walk your bike off the boardwalk right here, right now. If I see you on the boards today, on your bike again…"

He was talking to Fitz like he was a moron. It was a good thing this cop couldn't read *his* thoughts.

"Thank you, officer. I'm walking off, right now. See me walking?"

…you putz!

Down the ramp, to the street, Fitz went – surveying what he could of the boardwalk crowd. Dagger Man had vanished like a magic trick. He could have been on the avenue by now, his Harley already motoring toward his appointment. Fitz searched the blocks near the boardwalk street ramps, listened for the distinctive – *Va-room!* – of a motorcycle. He heard nothing. The guy was gone, and there seemed no way Fitz could share what he knew, without raising eyebrows.

Unless…

A demonstration! Yes, someone else could try on the bike helmet; maybe even a cop could hit the boards in 7th gear and listen to all that mental chatter for himself! The shore patrol station was nearby. If one cop believed him, if just one guy didn't think he was out of his mind…

*Maybe I **am** out of my mind.*

He chugged along the street, tapping the helmet's lightning bolt. Nothing happened. Not even FM 101 came through. He heard only dead air from the speakers.

"Damn..."

He had cheated death once, and for a while today, he believed he might do it again. But Mr. Death *(the insidious bastard!)* had bested him. Fitz could only return home, pretending none of this had happened – at least, until the evening news reported the grisly murder of some unsuspecting woman he didn't even know and was unable to save.

He pedaled Atlantic Avenue's bike lane. It wasn't a long distance back, maybe a twenty-minute ride...

***

...enough time to replay the day's insane events. Biking was a good way to clear his head. *All right, then...*

Well, who hadn't occasionally entertained thoughts that would shame them if discovered? How many grown men (like myself!) sneaked off to their laptops to watch Internet porn? Wouldn't want the wife reading those prurient thoughts, would we? Am I so different than that horny kid on the boardwalk? Hell, getting my hands on Dora's shapely ass had been my first thought the moment I met her. Of course, I told her the first thing that attracted me were her eyes.

Lies, good ones, bad ones...

Years earlier, hadn't he lied to his daughter when he accidentally backed the Camry over her kitten, insisting to ten-year-old Julie her pet must have run away? For weeks following that sorry episode, Fitz's guilt leaked through his veneer, like grease through a paper bag. He'd finally come clean, because some demons just wouldn't stay hidden...

***

...Like his shameful resentment of Dora's beauty – still

incredible enough to turn heads – while Fitz's mirror revealed a man aging considerably less than gracefully. His wife must have seen this: the years, chipping away at what remained of her husband's sex appeal. It was just like Dora to never say a word. Yes, that was another of his ugly little secrets, that idiotic insecurity, owing to his wife's unfading allure. Hell, there was probably an additional mountain of secret debris, buried deep inside Fitz's subconscious that only a shrink could uncover.

...Or someone able to read minds.

Probably, Dagger Man had been exercising some ol' Freudian Id, to clean out his own emotional sludge – those awful thoughts **everyone** *had locked inside their brain's darkest chambers. Maybe, to stay sane, the man had to fantasize a little insanity; had to shift into another gear.*

Fitz smiled at his own metaphor. Fantasizing bloody revenge didn't mean the man planned to *act* on it. The guy was just coping with his wounded ego, thinking terrible thoughts like the rest of the board walking crowd – and like the rest of the world. Fitz realized maybe he was rationalizing his own circumstances, looking for the escape clause from his own guilt, *but that was another way of coping too, wasn't it?* He made his decision. He would tell no one, and he would do nothing.

Close to home now, he tapped the helmet one last time. *Thank Christ,* Oldies 101 kicked in and not some poor schmuck's secret thoughts. Through the speakers, Connie Francis sang how her heart had a mind of its own. Pretty Connie was another young siren who gave the adolescent Fitz one huge bone-on, and wouldn't Dora appreciate that bit of information? Pedaling into his driveway, he left the racer in the garage with the helmet hanging on its handlebars. A few hours remained before dinner, *so maybe...*

"Dora? You home? Come see what I bought!"

No answer. His wife probably had gone shopping for some more Kale for another shitty salad. Maybe he had time to sneak a sandwich? – *Some roast beef piled thick and high, lots of pickles, a smear of mayo. One sandwich – how could that hurt?*

Fitz headed for the kitchen to create his masterwork; meat packed so high, the finished product barely fit into his mouth. Locating a bread knife, he sliced his snack into halves before practically attacking it. Exhausted from his biking excursion, Fitz had time for a short nap before Dora returned. He cleaned up all evidence of his dietary lapse and hit the couch.

Connie Francis sang his brain to sleep.

***

Kill the bitch! Kill her today!

Fitz didn't have a restful hour. That other mind, the one that lay *deeper* than his conscious one, had not exorcised those snarling demons as he had hoped. When he dragged himself from the couch it had turned dark, and he stretched to find the switch on the table lamp. What he saw took a moment to register. His mouth contorted, but no sound escaped, except the heavy breath that became his wife's name.

"Dora...!"

Like a discarded doll, his wife lay spread-eagled on the floor. The black bike helmet lay at her side, a severe dent embedded in one of its lightning bolts, that matched the discolored fracture Fitz saw in his woman's crushed skull.

"My God! My God!!"

Needing a moment to think clearly, Fitz realized he was clasping the bread knife. The serrated blade was dripping now, but not with mayonnaise. Dora's cut throat revealed thick gouts of blood leaking in an expanding pool on the carpet. Dark freckles of the stuff had spattered his clothes.

Dora...beaten with the helmet to the floor, her skull shattered, then her throat cut...

The knife fell from his hand. A lightning bolt of pain sent him crumbling to the carpet clutching his chest.

Try to cough. Read that somewhere. Just keep coughing, keep the blood circulating.

The blood...Dora...

Fitz had no breath to cough. He had no breath to breathe.

From the street came the sound of a motor starting up.

Va-roooom!!

Maybe a Harley?

Maybe...Maybe not.

The blood-soaked knife he had held, maybe placed into his hand...?

Worse than that, could he have...somehow...

...himself?

Impossible. Impossible!

Can't die...have to know the truth...have to know...

Dora...

"That ass you just pinched still has plenty of mileage."

His chest pain turned excruciating. He twitched and kicked on the floor.

Not fair! Death...not...

He reached for Dora's hand, held it close to him. Already, her flesh had gone cold. Looking into the dead eyes of his wife, Arthur Fitz knew his darkness would come soon. He found strength to mutter two words before it came.

"Insidious bastard..."

TAKE HER HOME
Gillian French

They blew past her on Old County Road, a skinny-shanks girl walking with a little boy.

Dooley reversed, whistling. Mason said, "Doo, for chrissake, don't." Four beers in the heat of the dugout had finished Mason. He wasn't up for the Sir Galahad routine.

Leaning out the window, Dooley called, "Hot out for walking." She came over. Dooley scarcely seemed to believe it—looked like he'd swallowed a bone—but recovered enough to say, "Plenty of room."

"There's two of us." She set the boy on her hip. The kid's face was full of fear.

In the cab, Mason tried to keep his knee away from hers. She was tall, with a dehydrated, sun-bleached look and some freckles. Couldn't be more than nineteen. She said her name was Ellie. Dooley gabbed to fill the silence, taking corners hard. "So. Ellie. Where were you walking to?"

"The river. We got so bug-bit that we decided to head home."

"Black flies. Get you every time. You must have sweet blood. Listen, you want to go swimming, I'll take you. The river isn't far."

Mason bit the inside of his cheek. He'd bawl Dooley out if it wouldn't be like snipping the guy's nutsack off in front of the girl. Great. Swimming. Cozy as hell. After he and Doo spent all morning doing their best to lose a softball game while swilling warm Pabst, Mason felt about a hair's breadth away from heaving in front of Miss Ellie, God, and everybody, and Dooley knew it. *Chowderhead.*

167

"What you think?" Ellie jiggled the boy on her lap. "Want to?" The boy folded his arms over his small chest. "It's all right," she said to Dooley. "He doesn't warm up to men."

Mason said, "We can drop you guys off." He bumped Ellie's knee and winced. Felicia would raise holy hell if she could see him right now. "Pick you up in a couple hours. No sweat."

"Right." Dooley snorted. "You and the little woman get to fooling around, and *I'll* be lucky to make it home before dark." Mason had moved in with Felicia a month ago, and suddenly he was a traitor to his buds and, "never hung out anymore", according to one Lawrence Edmund Dooley, Jr.

"Dude, seriously. I need a shower and a nap." Ellie and the boy were watching Mason. "Sorry."

Dooley wasn't listening. "Me and Mason work at the Home Depot in Augusta. Flooring. You?" He glanced at her. "You work?"

She set her chin on the boy's head. "I take care of him. His dad works at the mill."

Mason caught Dooley's eye. Now he'd turn around, for sure. Now he'd take her right home.

The silence stretched on. Greenery and sunshine flashed by outside.

"I always miss this damn turn-off," Dooley said. Mason rested his aching head against the doorframe.

The river road was dirt. There was nobody else parked along the banks. Ellie said, "We're here, baby," to the boy, who ran to the water. She followed.

Mason caught Dooley's arm. "Dude."

Dooley watched Ellie stepping out of her shorts. "I know, right?"

"Take. Her. Home. We don't need some pissed-off mill worker after us."

"Who's gonna tell him?"

"The kid. Think of that?"

Dooley grinned.

"Far as I can see, he doesn't talk."

Dooley went towards the long, tall expanse of Ellie in a tank suit. She continued down the banks. He trailed her. The boy waded up to his knees.

Mason sat in the sand. Dooley and Ellie went around the turn and there was the sound of them going up the slope into the woods. Insects hummed. The boy stood in the water, hands at his sides, staring up at the trees. Mason thought about calling him in, but didn't. Instead, he fell asleep.

***

In his dream, he could smell the stink of the river. The four of them still rode in Dooley's pickup, woods streaming by. There was no sound. Dooley's mouth moved endlessly. Mason saw Ellie's knee next to his own.

At once, it was nighttime. Beyond the windshield, only the headlights and the moon shone. Whatever sat beside him now made the hair on his arms bristle and his scrot shrivel.

They were looking at him. They were waiting. The stink was so bad, now. Nothing could've made Mason turn his head, but he knew without looking that whatever sat beside him was blackened, jaws agape, eyeballs missing. When they moved, it was with a sound like dried leaves ground under a boot.

***

Mason sat upright before he'd even opened his eyes and retched into the sand. The boy was still in the water, humming softly and skimming his hands over the surface.

When Dooley and Ellie returned, Doo hung a few paces back, hands in his pockets. Ellie went to the water.

Mason looked at Dooley. His gaze was down and he had two flushed spots on his cheeks. The guy had been hard up, sure, but Dooley didn't do embarrassed. Ever. "How was it?" Mason asked flatly.

Dooley wouldn't look up. "I dunno." He tried to find more words, shook his head.

Ellie dove into the water and swam. Dooley sat with his hands dangling and didn't say much. Mason didn't try to hurry him along, either. He checked his phone and saw four missed calls from Felicia. He could've called, explained why he still wasn't home, but the words seemed impossible. Ellie swam with a sweeping stroke, back and forth. She stopped and played with the boy, splashing and dipping him. His laughter echoed down the banks.

The sun sank, pooling fire on the horizon. Ellie put on her shorts and cover-up. "That felt good. Thanks." She and the boy were shadows holding hands. "He really wanted to go swimming today."

They all walked to the truck in silence.

***

Home for Ellie turned out to be a shack by Turner Crossing. Mason had noticed it before, mostly because of the trash in the yard. The porch light was on. Rafters of cigarette smoke hung around a silhouette sitting tipped back in a lawn chair. He was big, her mill worker.

Dooley stopped some distance up the road. The figure on the porch didn't move. If this guy was waiting up for his baby mama, he didn't seem too worried.

Ellie's son made a soft sound and pressed against her. Mason realized that the kid wasn't scared of him and Doo; he was scared, period.

"You shouldn't go in there." Dooley hardly sounded like himself.

Ellie didn't move.

"We could go anywhere. You could come to my place. My Ma will be there. She won't mind."

Mason stared at the shadow on the porch. More smoke rose.

"He gets real ugly." Ellie spoke evenly. "Always accusing me. Sometimes he says our boy isn't his."

Distantly, Mason thought *smart guy*, but it seemed beside the point with the boy trembling like that. "It's okay," Mason told him. The kid's eyes held the moonlight.

Dooley shook his head, shifting into gear. "Nossir. You should not go in there."

They drove past the house. The shadow never moved. Like he didn't even see them.

***

"Where do you want to go, Ellie? Anywhere you want to go," Dooley said.

The boy whimpered again. She held him tighter. After a moment: "His daddy's got a place up the road. Sets up his deer stand there."

"Won't he come looking for you?"

"No. Not now."

"But you can't hide out in the woods."

Her profile was black. "We need to go there."

Mason watched the moon ride the sky ahead of them, disbelieving. His phone vibrated. Felicia, wondering whether to be pissed-off or scared.

They parked on the shoulder. The woods were dense. There was almost no sign of a trail. How had Ellie spotted it so easily in the dark? Mason grabbed the Maglite from under the seat, because apparently, Dooley wasn't worried about being able to see: he trotted right out after Ellie, her lugging the boy on her hip. "Hey. Hold up, you guys," Mason called.

He fell in thigh-high weeds. By the time he retrieved the flashlight and stood, there was no sign of them. "Wait." Panic rolled over him, and he ran.

A flash of Dooley's white t-shirt winked through the trees. Dooley was calling Ellie's name. For a second, Mason thought he saw her—darting, clutching the boy—but when he aimed the light, she was gone again.

Mason didn't stop until he burst into a clearing. Good place for a deer stand. A ring of rocks remained from a campfire.

Dooley ran out of the bushes, gasping. "I lost her, man."

"Why the hell would she take off like that?"

Dooley yelled her name. No answer from the woods. "You think she's hurt or something?" His eyes were wild.

Mason walked around the clearing, swiping at the tall grass. *Why'd he gotten so revved-up in the first place? Friggin' Doo.*

***

The ground sloped away beyond the clearing, and Ellie stood at the bottom. She wasn't there, and then she was, holding the boy. Mason didn't speak. He kept the light trained on her. Both she and the boy held his gaze, and then she turned and stepped into the darkness, her legs long and deer-like.

Mason started down the slope and wiped out hard in loose soil. The *stink*. Rich and crackling, strong as in the dream. He scrambled for the flashlight. Faintly, he heard Doo, say, "You okay?"

The beam showed fresh grass growing from the mound he'd sunken into. An animal had been at the soil, digging down to whatever smelled so rotten and edible beneath the surface. Through the earth, blackened fingers flashed bony tips.

Mason became aware that Dooley stood behind him. He was frozen in the act of helping Mason up, his gaze locked on the fingers, his mouth open.

***

From the *Kennebec Journal*, pg. 1:

DUDLEY TOWNSHIP— Police have made an arrest in the case of a woman and child whose bodies were discovered in a shallow grave in the woods off Turner Crossing three weeks ago. Trevor Witham, 29, of Dudley, confessed to the murder of his common-law wife, Eleanor Chapel, 20, originally of Somerset County, and their 4-year-old son, Michael, both of whom, Witham told relatives had left the area. The bodies were found a short distance from Witham's home on August 5th. According to police, on May 22nd, following an argument the night before in which Chapel threatened to move out, Witham trailed mother and son down Turner Crossing in the direction of Little River, where the two had planned a day trip. After getting them into his vehicle, he drove them to the wooded area and stabbed them both multiple times in the chest and throat. He then buried the bodies.

Witham's confession removes suspicion from two men who found the bodies, Laurence Edmund Dooley, Jr., 24, and Mason Gedrick, 24, who police originally believed to be involved in the crime. While Dooley could not be reached for comment, Gedrick told the *Journal*, "Now she (Chapel) can have some peace." How Dooley and Gedrick located the bodies remains unclear, but police no longer— (cont'd pg. 3)

LONG MAN
Mike Thorn

I think it must've been the sound that woke me up. That heavy, slurping sound, like a saucy noodle slithering its way into a mouth.

I rolled over toward the noise's source, and the thing that I saw shocked my groggy senses.

There was something like a man in the mirror. Not in front of the mirror, but *in* the mirror. In front of the mirror was the impression of empty space, but I could see the rustling of carpet, as if something was stirring there. I could see the steady snowfall and buildup of detritus.

Terror incites paralysis at moments like these.

I could only watch with my mouth stretched open, a failing effort to cry out, to produce any sound at all.

And he watched. He watched me with eyes that were not like eyes, gazing without seeing, an unblinking and unearthly nightwatch. I saw the deathly skin that ringed his pinpoint eyes, skin too thin for eyelids, and I watched his mouth as it gnawed and chewed, forming infected holes lined redly with flesh that dangled, wet and raw, that hung and swayed in strips from its— not its, from *his*—face. His fingers picked at a naked torso; no genitals, but I knew it was a he, and flakes of tummy-flesh came off, drifting to form ashen puddles on the carpet.

I told myself that it was a nightmare, and I tried again to scream, but could not find the strength, and I rolled over to face the wall. I cried, and I tried to sleep.

I was only six-years-old, after all. How was I supposed to deal with something like that?

Long Man

***

The Long Man visited every night for a month, and even when I turned away, I could hear his rasping, ragged breath and the meaty sound of teeth tugging flesh.

Every morning, I'd sit dead-eyed at the table, and my father would urge me to hurry up or I'd miss the bus.

I often considered telling him about my nightly visitor.

Eventually, after thirty nights—or maybe more, the weeks started to bleed into each other at some point—I told my parents. They didn't laugh. They calmly talked to me about nightmares, and the power of imagination, and they told me that monsters weren't real; that monsters would go away if I just didn't believe in them.

I tried so hard not to believe, but this monster had no intention of going anywhere.

I couldn't rest until a year later, when my parents—by now exasperated with my hysterical rantings about the man in the mirror, and even more exasperated by the ballooning cost of child psychiatrists—finally took action. The mirror in my room was a family heirloom, and they had no intention to dispose of it, no matter *what* I saw inside of it. First, they moved it to another room and replaced it with a new, inexpensive model.

The new mirror brought the same nighttime visitations.

One exhausted summer morning, my mother finally tore the new mirror from its wall mount, slammed it deliberately into the backseat of her car and drove it to the landfill. I went with her, and I still remember the sensation of cold and papery fingertips on the back of my neck as we drove away. I whipped my head around to make sure the mirror was gone, and I saw it tilted atop a pile of rubbish, emaciated gulls circling its cracked and dimly-shimmering face.

He was gone.

By then, my child's mind had given him a name: the Long Man.

***

It took me nearly two decades and a lot of whiskey to tell my best friend, Donny, about the shape that had haunted my bedroom mirror as a child. I expected him to shake his head and say something along the lines of, "that's real fucked up, man—nothing like a kid's imagination, right?"

Donny said no such thing. Instead, he seemed to forget that he was in the process of pouring another shot. He just poured and poured, his eyes fixed on some arbitrary spot on the wall, the whiskey spilling across the tabletop and dribbling off to pool on the carpet.

"No," he said. "Jesus fucking Christ, no."

"Donny," I said, grabbing hold of his forearm.

To say he was shaking would be like saying he enjoyed a drink on occasion, and Donny was a full-on, bona-fucking-fide alcoholic. The muscles on his arm were spasming under my fingers, his entire body violently rattling.

"*Donny*," I said again, and he hollered with shock as if awoken from a hyper-realistic nightmare. His arm flung and the bottle sailed from his hand, smashing against the wall behind him.

He turned to fix a stare on me, seeming to forget that he had marinated my living room with Maker's Mark mere seconds ago.

"Long, that's right," he said. "Not tall, but *long*. Yes, I remember him. The *Long Man*."

"Yeah, he looked sort of…stretched," I added.

"Like the skin was being pulled tight across his bones. Like he only grew up and up and up, like the shadow of a person."

"Yes," I said, and then, after a pause, "Only…how do you know?"

"Because he lived in my mirror, too," Donny said, a manic and humorless smile flickering on his face.

"But, how? How could he—"

"—Be in two places at once? No. No, he couldn't," Donny said. "He only showed up when my parents moved me into the

176

basement bedroom. They wanted to convert my old room into a guest suite, and guess what? There was a mirror in the basement room."

My whole body was goose-fleshed. I'd already forgotten about the booze now soaking into the white carpet and staining the walls. All I could focus on was Donny's faraway stare, and the fact that I could almost *see* the Long Man haunting his eyes.

"For me, it started with the sound," Donny said. "Squelching. Like a dog pulling gristle from a bone. I thought maybe it was mice living in the walls, or bad plumbing maybe…What the hell does a seven-year-old kid know, right?"

"Seven," I said.

Of course. It made sense. Donny was a year older than me. It seemed that the Long Man couldn't have more than one host at a time—if hosts is what we were—and he also seemed to have a fondness for young boys; a fondness for watching them in their bedrooms.

Alone. At night.

"Did you ever see him disappear?" I knew the answer before I even put the question forward.

"No. There was always a blackness…like a rush of forced sleep…so quick. And I'd wake up—fuck, this is embarrassing—but, I'd wake up in a puddle of my piss. Usually crying, but not always. Nosebleeds too, most of the time. Just lying there in my piss and blood. And my dad would come in, you know, and he'd see the pile of skin on the floor and he'd see the mess in my bed and he'd just say, 'for Christ's sake, not again,' like the whole thing was *my* fault, right? And I'd say, 'Dad, how could I make that mess on the floor while I'm here in bed?' The theories my parents came up with were endless."

"Bad ventilation," I said, and it was only just then that I remembered my own parents' half-baked rationalization for the perpetual, ashy stain in front of the mirror. "Build-up in the furnace vents."

"I heard that one, too." Donny laughed, once. "Buildup of moisture in the walls. Flaking paint."

"Rotting stucco."

"Now *that one* I never heard."

And so, I learned that night, for certain, that the Long Man *was* real, no matter what my army of childhood psychiatrists might've urged to the contrary. But the discovery was far from comforting. Instead, it gave me the sense that the Long Man might still be out there, waiting for the right time. Waiting for a mirror.

***

He'd never actually *done* anything—I'd long since reasoned the bedwetting, the nosebleeds, and the blackouts to be the products of powerful fits, although, I was starting to doubt that, now.

I found it fair to assume that the Long Man was hungry. Why else was he watching? Why else, that constant gnawing and tearing at his own face, and that heavy, awful breathing?

Donny slept on my sofa that night. I pretended to pass out on the armchair beside him. Truth be told, I didn't sleep at all.

I just didn't want to go into my bedroom alone. Never mind the fact that I didn't, and would never again, have a mirror there.

It might sound unbelievable, but the topic never arose between Donny and me again. Not until the night it all happened, at least…but I'll get to that soon.

It was almost as if Donny and I believed that we could will the Long Man into nonexistence, simply by ignoring the memories. By avoiding them. By repressing them.

The nasty thing about memories is, as the tried-and-true cliché says, they can come back to haunt you.

And sometimes memories have teeth.

***

One night, in December, our friend, Cody, drove us to a dingy but cheap nightclub called Studio 73. It was one of those nights when the cold wind seems to cut through your flesh and coil your bones. We thought a drink (or two, or three, or more) would be as good a way as any to help warm us up.

We pulled into the parking lot, and Donny, in the backseat, leaned toward Cody and me.

"Did we ever tell you about the *thing*?" he asked Cody. "The fucking man-*thing* that used to show up in our mirrors in the nighttime? That would stare at us, night after night after night, and *chew* its fucking face open? Did we ever tell you about that?"

His voice sounded so flat, so unbalanced, and it wasn't just from the weed we'd been smoking earlier that night. The memories of the Long Man haunted both Donny and I, constantly, but tonight—the haunting was on Donny, big-time.

Cody turned to me, sitting in the passenger seat. I avoided his eyes and rotated to look at Donny.

"Donny, come on, man," I said. "Let's not talk about this. It's weird. Let's just go have fun, all right?"

"Did we *tell* you, Cody?" Donny asked, louder this time.

"Uh, no...I don't believe you did," Cody said with a stilted chuckle, shifting in his seat.

"I could hear it breathing, and you could, too. Couldn't you?" Donny looked at me.

My heart machine-gunned. I never wanted to think about the Long Man again, least of all, when my mind was toasted from too much THC and alcohol.

"*Couldn't you?*"

"Yes," I said. "Yes, I could hear him."

"And this thing, this...*man-thing* was pale white, like ashes, wasn't he?" Donny continued. "Yes," (he answered for me), "and it would just *stare* and rip at its own cheeks with its teeth, and I could see the discolored infections spreading across its face. And its eyes were blank. Totally blank."

"His," I said. Nobody spoke, and so, I said it again. "*His.* The Long Man is a *he.*"

Cody glanced, first at me, and then at Donny. "Why are you guys talking about this right now? Is this some kind of fucked up joke? You're freaking the living hell out of me, man. Jesus."

Donny stared ahead, his eyes wide and wet, like a scolded puppy's, and he said something almost inaudible that I think might've been, "*here*."

"What?" Cody asked.

"*Because he's here right now*," Donny said, quivering visibly, tears now rolling down his cheeks. "*He's sitting right beside me.*"

I twisted around again to see the empty space beside him, and I thought, *Good God, Donny has lost it. The Long Man has taken his mind and fucked it up for good. Donny's gone.*

It didn't take long for the thought to dawn on me, though, and I said it aloud: "The mirror."

Cody and I cast our eyes to the rear view mirror, in unison, and I saw exactly what I knew I would see.

I saw *him*.

I saw his naked, mottled body. His ribs poked through a veil of tissue. Tattered strips of skin drooped from the gashes chewed into his cheeks. He was raining blood from the facial lesions, splattering the floor of Cody's van.

There was this eerie pause; a moment of utter silence, and then I realized that the radio was still playing—that song, "*Believe*," by Cher. It was just about to hit the chorus at that moment.

And then, Donny started screaming.

Not yelling or crying, just flat out, fucking *screaming*. I turned away from the mirror to look at him, and his neck was being pulled toward the roof—pulled so far that it looked like some kind of gruesome taffy—and then his head pulled free with a nauseating squelch, and his scream cut short with that sound. His head swung, in midair, over his ragged, spouting neck; blood pumping and spewing. Then his chest pulled open, and I could see his ribs being pried apart. I could see his heart, all wet and red, and I became suddenly aware that Cody was just watching

180

with a vacant face. He couldn't seem to register the scene with any degree of emotion or understanding.

I was frozen as well, watching Donny—my friend—pull apart. Watching him being *pulled apart.*

The parts that came off were suspended; I could only bear one more glance in the mirror, that was it...and I could see that the Long Man was *chewing* on him. He was finally getting the meal that he'd waited for so long, and there was blood smeared all over his face.

***

I snapped. I mean: I completely lost it. I unbuckled my seatbelt and, with fumbling fingers, I yanked the back door open and I just threw Donny—Donny's remains, more like it—out into the parking lot.

Cody floored it. He peeled out of there, and the radio was playing so loudly that I couldn't tell whether he was screaming or laughing but, judging by his face, he could've been doing either. Or both.

***

When Cody drove me home that night, I'd already made the decision to leave. I won't tell you where I came from, and I won't tell you where I've gone. The investigation must be well underway by now...or maybe they're already looking for me. Maybe they've been looking for a long time. I hope that Cody got away safe, but I couldn't stick around to find out. It was too much of a risk.

You might think I'm a real bastard for doing what I did, for running away, and maybe I am—but I doubt that any one of you would have known what else to do.

Don't ask me what's happened since then. I don't read the papers. I don't even use the Internet anymore.

All I know is that no police officer in the world would believe that sometimes a thing called the Long Man decides to show up in a little boy's bedroom mirror, that he waits for the right moment and then finally...he *feeds*.

The Long Man must've found a new host, by now. If not, I imagine he's getting pretty hungry. I don't know how much I've aged since all of this happened.

I cannot, after all, look at my own reflection. No, I don't believe I'll ever do that again.

SOLITARY
Kerry G.S. Lipp

Shaw shanked him in the middle of the cafeteria for his cookie. No one else saw, and as Thurgood poised to retaliate, a guard was all over him.

"Trust me, Thurgood, you don't want to do this," the screw said, leading Thurgood Nelson by the elbow back to his cell. A small trickle of blood leaked from Thurgood's hand.

"Shaw started it. Fucking stabbed me for my cookie," Thurgood spat.

"Yeah, I know, but no one else saw and believe it or not, I'm actually trying to help you."

"Help me?" Thurgood shook his head.

"I'm serious," the guard said. "We've got a new solitary ward we're just itching to try out. Let 'em try it on someone else. Trust me, you don't want to be the first. And I promise you, once you hear about it, you'll forget all about this."

"Maybe," Thurgood shrugged and entered his cell.

The drab, grey walls of his standard cell welcomed him. Uncomfortable, small, disgusting, but at least he had it to himself. He called the fourth floor of the west cellblock home, and would for most of his future.

Thurgood Nelson got locked up for good after confronting a group of six in a seedy bar after getting hustled in a pool game. He stood over all six with a broken cue and a bloody nose, and was too busy kicking the biggest guy in the head to even realize what he'd done until three cops had him pinned down and cuffed.

According to the report at his trial, all in all, he'd broken over a hundred of their bones, spilled close to ten pints of blood, and the number of stitches needed to sew his victims up hit quadruple digits. Though outnumbered, kicking the shit out of them that bad bought him no sympathy from a jury.

Shouts across the block brought him back to the present.

"Fuck you man, don't fucking look at me, don't fucking talk to me!"

Thurgood walked to the opening of his cell and faced the argument. Two guys on the opposite side stood nose-to-nose.

Thurgood didn't know both their names, but the bigger of the two, he knew, was named Murphy. Murphy grabbed the smaller one by the throat and threw him over the railing, down four stories onto unforgiving concrete.

"Holy fuck," Thurgood whispered.

The cellblock burst out in cheers.

A siren sounded and a brigade of guards stormed the block.

The guards swarmed Murphy, who stood, red-faced and sweating, looking down at the splattered body at the bottom of the landing. The mass of guards clobbered him with their batons and didn't stop until well after Murphy collapsed.

A couple of guards stalked through, making sure all the prisoners and the cells were accounted for while others dragged Murphy away.

More cheers and catcalls from the prisoners. The air felt electric. People died here often, but Thurgood had never witnessed a blatant murder right before his eyes.

"Jesus," he muttered, running his fingers across the paint-chipped bars confining him.

***

A week passed and no one had seen or heard from Murphy. Rumors circulated that the guards had beaten him to death. Prisoners grilled Murphy's cellmate for an update, but he'd just shrug and say, "The fuck am I supposed to know?"

Almost as disturbing as Murphy's absence was the stain at the bottom of the cellblock. Janitors scrubbed and scrubbed, but the dead man's blood and brains still tainted the floor like oil in a garage. Like a memento to the residents of Mansfield Reformatory, reminding them that they could all die at any moment.

Things stayed quiet for that week, but a lot of the population was transferred to the infirmary, which had turned into a makeshift tuberculosis ward. In there, people coughed themselves to death and disappeared. Going there was like going to a leper colony. It no longer became a matter of if, but when. Death and disease filled the corridors of the prison, lurking like fog around every corner at any second.

Thurgood, like most prisoners, forgot all about Murphy.

Until he showed back up.

He returned with a few cuts and bruises. What bothered Thurgood, wasn't the stitches on the bridge of Murphy's crooked nose or the sick yellow of healing bruises, it was the deadness in the man's eyes. All the fight, the fire, the piss and vinegar had drained out and Thurgood guessed that Murphy might've been the first one to check in at the new solitary hotel.

Thurgood wanted to ask, but never got the chance.

In the middle of the night, the same night he reappeared, Murphy jumped over the railing with a bed sheet noosed around his neck. With a cell directly across, the first thing Thurgood saw upon waking was Murphy's blackening face and swaying body.

News of more deaths in the tuberculosis ward trickled down and the cellblock stayed mostly silent for a few days. It seemed like there was nowhere to hide from death.

More and more inmates got quarantined for tuberculosis, including neighbors on both sides of Thurgood. He felt fine, but he was scared to cough. The absence of so many prisoners did clear some of the stink out and gave those that remained a little extra breathing room.

As the halls thinned out, one person Thurgood saw more and more often was Shaw. Thurgood's hair-trigger temper had cooled and Shaw had even apologized. Even prisoners needed some comfort and camaraderie as the population died and disappeared all around them.

One day, Shaw sat next to Thurgood at lunchtime. Though they'd made amends, Thurgood still felt himself tense up as the other man took a chair. Shaw nodded, and Thurgood nodded back.

"Hey," Shaw said.

"Hey," Thurgood said.

They each ate in silence for a few moments.

"You here for a reason? Or is it just my lovely company?"

"Well, you're one of the last familiar faces I know around here. Seems everyone else is either dead or dying or just... gone."

"True enough," Thurgood said.

"Plus, all these people dying, I feel extra guilty about a lotta the shit I done to good people," he gestured to Thurgood's hand. Then he offered him pick of anything on his plate.

"I'm good. We're good," Thurgood said.

"I got something else to say," Shaw said.

"I'm listening."

"Look man, you see 'em carting people out every day. They never come back. They aren't letting them go. People are taking sick and people are dying. It's only a matter of time until the death and disease decide to creep up on us."

"Probably," Thurgood shrugged.

"And that doesn't bother you? Doesn't that scare the shit out of you?"

"I mean, sure, but I've accepted it. I'm locked up for at least a few more years. I ain't going nowhere. I just go to bed and wake up and put one foot in front of the other and I hope for the best. That nasty shit's contagious one way or another and you can't hide from it. Worrying? That'll just make you another kind of sick."

Shaw chewed his food, listening.

"What if there was a way to hide from it?" Shaw asked.

"Unless you know something I don't know, there ain't."

"I do."

"You got an escape plan?"

"Can you just let me finish?"

Thurgood nodded.

"Just before the tuberculosis outbreak, they put in a new part of the prison. A prison for the prisoners, you could call it."

Thurgood remembered the screw talking him out of going there.

"It's called solitary confinement. They lock you up in there; small, dark room, no light, no windows, feed you through a slot."

"I heard about it. Sounds awful," Thurgood said.

"It is. Drove Murphy so damned crazy that even when he got out of there, he took his own life."

Neither man spoke as that reality *hung* in the air for a minute.

"Must've been horrible," Thurgood finally said.

"So is tuberculosis," Shaw said. "I think this is the only shot we've got. How long you think you could hold out in solitary without losing your shit?"

"I...I don't know," Thurgood said. "I used to live alone. Spent a lot of time alone, but the option to go out was always there."

"Yeah, well, I'm willing to take my chances in solitary. This place shrinks a little more every day, the way it is. I need an answer, cowboy."

Thurgood looked around the cafeteria, almost down by a third. Even the number of guards was down and the remaining looked scared or wore masks.

"Yeah," he said. "I'm in."

"All right," Shaw said and slipped him something across the table.

Thurgood looked down at the shank in his hand.

"I guess you owe me one," Shaw smiled. "Make it look good. Just stick me somewhere that won't hurt me too bad."

"When?"

"Soon as we finish eating. Don't know what they serve down there. This might be our last good meal for a while."

Shaw swallowed his last bite and gave Thurgood a quick nod. Thurgood clenched his jaw, white-knuckling the shank, but he didn't act.

"Do it," Shaw said through clenched teeth.

The bell rang, indicating the end of the lunch period. Guards would be escorting them back to their cells any second.

"Goddamn it!" Shaw yelled. Then louder, "Fuck you!" He jumped to his feet and circled Thurgood's throat with his hands. Their cafeteria chairs toppled over, spilling both men to the floor.

"Do it," Shaw whispered into his ear as fellow prisoners crowded around and guards came running.

Thurgood squeezed the shank and drove it straight into Shaw's skin. He stabbed three times, puncturing the meat of Shaw's bicep, thigh, and buttocks. Shaw screamed in pain and tightened his grip on Thurgood's neck, as Thurgood's face turned bright red.

Just as Shaw released Thurgood's neck for fear of killing him, a mob of prison guards knocked him off and clubbed them both with batons.

To really sell it, both men fought and struggled against the guards and restraints, spitting insults. Thurgood's face retained its natural color as trickles of blood bloomed through Shaw's prison uniform. Before their escorts led them separate ways, the two locked eyes and flashed matching grins for a job well done.

***

Solitary sucked. It was, indeed, exactly what he thought it would be, but even so, no one could prepare for those conditions.

First, the space. Thurgood's tiny cinderblock cell confined him, restricted his ability to stretch to full wingspan. The rough walls provided no comfort and he spoke to himself to keep his sanity, but before long, the sound of his own voice haunted him.

Second, the darkness. Thurgood could not see his hands. The inky darkness swallowed them and felt more like a black hole than something of this earth.

Third, the smell. No air flowed through the cell and every smell was intensified in the absence of anything else. Between his own odor and that of his waste, he thought he'd be thankful for the smell of the food at mealtime. But instead, the stench tinged the aroma of the food to the point that he could taste it as he ate.

Fourth – and the thing that compounded everything else: the heat. Though an Ohio winter dug its claws in outside of Mansfield Reformatory, the solitary ward felt like a forge. The dark, dirty cell provided no escape from the heat that covered everything like a blanket. No breeze, no air, nothing but strangling, dark, dirty, stinky, heat.

His imagination provided no relief. Instead of plunging into the endless depths of the human mind, Thurgood flipped through all the boneheaded things he'd done in his life; bets he'd lost, women he'd dropped, family and friends he'd hurt. After that, his present flashed through his mind and he saw clear images of all the brutal prison beatings he'd witnessed and a realistic picture of all the infected, coughing themselves to death up in the tuberculosis ward.

Those thoughts stole Thurgood's breath and he tried to catch it, but the rancid air did nothing but send him into a fit of violent coughing. He couldn't get himself under control. When the hyperventilating subsided, he tried to worm more productive thoughts into his head.

How long did they say he'd be in solitary?

Seven days.

How long had he already been in solitary?

Shit. He didn't know. No sunrise, no sunset – nothing but void – made it impossible to tell. But then he had an idea; three meals a day, times seven days, equaled 21 meals.

He counted his meals and almost choked.

Five.

Not even a quarter of the way there.

What have I done?

Again, images of prisoners infected with tuberculosis played through his mind. All the coughing – hacking up phlegm and blood – and the fevers and the madness; but at least death provided a way out – and the dying, at least, had the comfort of companionship with others.

Thurgood had nothing.

With those thoughts fluttering through his head, Thurgood drifted off to sleep.

***

Nightmares.

Visions of the dead and dying surrounded him, walking through the walls of the impossible darkness. Diseased corpses coughed infected sprays of blood and mucus into Thurgood's face.

He gasped himself into consciousness and screamed himself into fits of coughing. Thurgood shrieked his throat raw and fell to his knees hacking up blood and sputum.

A screech of creaky metal, sliding, revealed the bright lights of the outside, and a guard said, "Dinner time, Nelson," and slid some food in. The guard leaned down, peered in and saw Thurgood coughing up blood; saw it drooling from the sides of his mouth and hanging from his chin.

"Fuck!" the guard yelled. "Anderson, get over here, Nelson's got tuberculosis!"

Another guard looked in.

"Well, I'll be damned," Anderson said.

"What do we do?"

"I don't want that shit," Anderson said. "And, if he's got it, he's already dead, anyways."

"We can't just leave him in there."

"Uh, yeah we can," Anderson said. "Dead men aren't contagious."

Thurgood tried to speak but his ruined throat betrayed him. He just burbled up more blood.

"Jesus. Look at him."

"Trust me," Anderson said, "These men are prisoners – Animals, *especially* the ones in solitary. Stop feeding him. Just let him die. Let the disease take him. We'll bag him and tag him, and we'll go home to our families without any threat of tuberculosis."

"You're right," the guard said. "Enjoy your last meal, Mr. Nelson."

And he slid the slot shut.

***

With the blackness once again taking hold, Thurgood screamed and screamed and it took him longer than his allotted seven days in solitary before he finally starved to death.

CREEPER IN THE CORN
James Coplin

It was 95 degrees, the humid air so still over the delta bottomlands that it draped Greensborough County like a sodden blanket. In Mississippi, in the summer, that's how it was. Yet, this year it was hot – hot as anybody's grandpa could remember. "Hot enough for y'all?" replaced, "Good Morning," as the common greeting; with a cold glass of sweet tea, as welcome as a bit of breeze.

Yet, whatever breeze might be, it never touched within the corn. In there, it was airless, dusty; so breathless that the weight of it pressed on a person's chest like a boot heel. That summer, forcing one's way through the dead air took as much effort as pushing aside the stalks, eyes stinging with sweat and pressed tight as a tick in endless acres of corn.

Will Buckman was the one that crashed through the corn on the last day of his life, June 7th, 1921. The sharp edges of the leaves snatched at the black and white stripes of his prison jumpsuit and the rasp and clatter of leg irons marked his position as he ran. Bloodhounds bayed behind him and he could hear the excited shouts of the pursuing Chain Gang guards and Deputies as they narrowed his lead. If he didn't find his way out of the corn right quick, they'd have him, and if they got him, it would do him no good just to put up his hands and surrender. And now, they were on him, hot as hornets, and getting closer.

He struggled through the tight, packed rows – panicky – not knowing any direction but up and down. Then, suddenly, and with no warning, he pushed out to open field; the rows ended as if snipped off with a shear.

Not too far off, was the porch and planked walls of some sharecropper's farmhouse. Even closer, lay a ramshackle, tottering Corn Crib; door unlatched and, from appearances, empty. It wasn't more than a hundred yards off. At least he could bar it against the dogs and make a stand. If they were man enough to come in after him, he bet less of them than came in would go out. Yes, Sirie – He was Bad Will Buckman, and if he was going down, they would be talking about it from Hell to next Tuesday!

In fact, it didn't go quite the way he expected – not at all.

Once the bloodhounds tracked him to the shed, the Guards and the Sheriff's boys just stood back a safe distance, leveled their twelve gauge's, and stood, blasting away, until the shed slats were no more than sawdust and splinters.

They shot Bad Will Buckman, dead as pulled pork, and then sat around smoking cigarettes and slapping each other on the back, as Joe Tobbers, the poor sharecropper who owned the place, waved his arms and complained of the damage.

"Now, Joe," Sheriff Payson dismissed the subject, as he rolled a tobacco chaw in his cheek, "Seems un-neighborly to expect the Parish to pay out hard cash for a no account shed that was falling down in the first place. Seems you should be grateful we got that murdering skunk a 'fore he had a chance to kill you and your boy and Missus. That fella was a bad one. Killed three other fellas up in Jacksonville, I heard tell, and scooted the head of a chain gang guard not an hour ago. You having to do a little carpentering to set things right, seems a small price to pay."

So, by-and-by, the prison wagon arrived, the bodily remains of Bad Will Buckman, tossed inside; with Joe Tobbers and his boy, Joe Junior, watching the dust recede down the road.

"Don't that beat all!" Joe Senior spat in disgust. "Well, boy, you can quit your gawkin'. Seems we've a heap of work to do."

With that, he stomped off; the boy at his heels, gazing with fascination at the fist-sized holes in the slats of the ruined Corn Crib, and spent shells littering the dooryard.

With Pa in his mood, it wouldn't do to show it, but, to a fourteen-year-old boy, the whole thing had been pretty danged exciting. But Pa was right about one thing: they'd been left a mess all right – stored straw bales blown to pieces and sacks of chicken feed spilled all over the floor. Already, the shed was buzzing with flies – red, thick as paint, dripping down the slats and the plank beneath their boots, pooled and slippery. So, Joe Junior – JJ – wheeled in a manure cart and was just starting to fork the soiled straw in when his Pa snarled at him.

"Boy! What the Hell you think you're doing? Leave that be."

JJ looked up, puzzled, hesitating in mid pitch.

"But, Daddy; it's spoiled. Got blood all over it and it will get stinking quick enough."

"So what? Straw's dear, at two bits a bale! You think I'm tossing money away? Y'all just rake it in a pile and set the worst of it aside. It will serve to bed pigs, and what's left, I'll use to put up a new scarecrow in the east field."

So, by-and-by, what had been spilled from the veins of the murderer, Bad Will Buckman, ended stuffed in the cast offs of a Mississippi dirt farmer.

***

Coincidental or not, everyone agreed it an uncommonly frightful scarecrow. It was only straw-stuffed, burlap bags, built around crossed sticks – padded arms set wide, tipped with old canvass gloves with the fingers worn through. The head was a meal sack, topped with Joe Tobbers' mule-stomped plug hat. Mrs. Tobbers had taken some caps off of coke bottles and sewn them on for eyes and lips. When the light caught them right, they seemed to wink; a pair of red pupils rimmed with silver. More than one passerby got the shivers, walking by in the twilight and seeing that crooked, bottle cap grin looking down like a mouthful of serrated teeth.

Joe dressed it in a rag of an old frock coat and pegged it up twelve feet high, looming above the tops of the corn, where it seemed to float like some watchful pagan idol. There, it twisted and turned in the breeze, coat tails flapping and bottle cap eyes unblinkingly surveying the corn.

One thing it did; it sure scared crows. At first, they wheeled cautiously above it, but soon, no crow would come within an acre of it. JJ noticed it first and something else. He mentioned it to his folks one morning as they sat at the breakfast table.

"Saw a passel of dead crows in the field, yesterday. Maybe a dozen or more. I hope it ain't bird fever. We better keep an eye on the chickens."

There was another peculiarity about their new scarecrow. It seemed unwilling to stay up the post.

The first time it went missing, they found it about a quarter mile up County Road 93, lying, face-down, in the drainage ditch. It was a puzzle as to how it got there, but Joe Senior recollected there were thunder storms that evening and opinioned that the wind could have twisted it off its peg. It was likely one of those thieving packs of dogs got at it and dragged it down the road, though, why they would do that and carry it so far, no one could fathom.

Joe Junior just said, "Yes, Daddy. I reckon that's what happened," but stood scratching his head and thinking. It was true the county was overrun with half-wild dogs, but they didn't bother much with what they couldn't eat. Nor was the scarecrow worried at or torn up. In the end, he just shrugged his shoulders and helped his Daddy carry it back to be hung up again on the peg.

Yet, three nights later, his Pa's explanation seemed the likelier when he was woken up by something crashing through the fields. He listened to the snap of broken stalks. Something heavy was deep in the corn, probably deer.

JJ knew that a foraging deer did more damage than twenty raccoons, so he got up, got dressed. He fetched his deer rifle and a pocket full of shells; picked up his kerosene lantern and set off to track the varmint. His Daddy would be pleased not only with him taking responsibility for the crop, but maybe, laying some venison on the table as well.

In the yard, the late night moon hung full and bright, bathing the surrounding corn tops in silvery beams. Yet, ten feet into the corn, it became dark and close as a briar patch. The yellow light of the lantern was lost outside a half-dozen paces ahead; the corn stalks shivered and rustled as his passage disturbed them and the night breeze above sighed like ghosts whispering down a chimney pipe.

It was hard to keep one's bearings. He could see the top of the post, now and again, through the swaying tassels, and used that to navigate. Yet, the closer he got, the more puzzled he became. It just didn't look right. *Something* was wrong, but it was dark and hard to see through the patchwork of leaves. Yet, as he reached the foot of it, he drew short, his jaw dropping open as he mentally rubbed his eyes, to be sure they saw what they did – or what they *didn't.*

The post was bare. Nothing hung upon it. Nothing lay down by its base.

Now, if it were daylight, he might have convinced himself of a logical reason. Yet, it was deep, dark night, and he was alone, in a whispering ocean of close-packed corn rows. The fact was, he was scared and scared good. What his imagination suggested, left small comfort in the rifle he almost forgot he carried. He didn't exactly turn and run, but if he were a horse, they would have called it a trot.

Worse, he was sure something was *moving* along with him. He could hear it, just out of sight; the sound of stalks being shuffled aside and footsteps crushing the dried leaves on the ground. They were picking up speed – moving closer – and JJ let out a shout, as something solid and heavy burst through the corn, just in front of him. It kept on going – the crushed stalks snapping, receding away in the dark. Yet, he'd seen just enough – the flash of brown fur, white tail and antlers. He almost wept with relief.

Deer!

Yet, there were no further thoughts of hunting it. JJ still had a whopping case of the jitters and the only cure he knew was to get safe at home, covers pulled over his head. Yet, which way was home? He'd been totally turned around by now. From what he could see of the stars, the deer had been heading north, towards the road. He thought it smart to do the same, coming out in the clear and following it back to his Daddy's cabin.

He walked along, lantern held low to pick up the trail. Somewhere up ahead, there was a quick, harsh cry that startled him; some night bird he supposed, though he'd never heard one like that before. It wasn't repeated.

He almost tripped over the thing sprawled on the trail, before his lantern caught it. It was the deer. It lay broken, twisted, with its head and wide, brown eyes lolling backwards over its shoulder. There wasn't a mark on it, but it was dead – still twitching. Yet, as JJ looked it over, he felt his stomach curl up like a corn snake. Caught here and there, in its fur, were wisps of old straw and a clump of it dangled from the point of an antler.

There, in the tiny circle of light, he forced himself to swivel his head towards where the post rose up from the field. As he knew it would be, it was no longer unoccupied. The scarecrow was back on it, now twisting in the air, so it faced JJ, across the field. The gloved hand seemed to wave at him, the bottle cap lips, grinning like a conspirator.

Don't worry, it seemed to whisper to him, in his thoughts. *The crop's safe. Everything is taken care of. We'll just keep our little secret between us, and the corn. Ain't that so, boy?*

And JJ did. He made it home, went back to bed and in the morning, said nothing about it to his folks or at any time after. But nothing, not even the threat of one of his Daddy's whippings, ever got him back into that field.

***

Displaying unexpected sensitivity, Joe Senior never pressed the issue. The fact was, there was little need.

Throughout High Summer and into Harvest Fall, that corn field prospered. Any weed daring to take root there withered and died. Not a single leaf was touched by canker or corn blight; not one kernel lost to varmints or pests. The cobs grew so fat and heavy, Mrs. Tobbers commented they looked like they'd butter themselves, and there was no little envy among the Tobbers' neighbors.

Joe Tobbers put it down as the long-deserved reward of a God fearing man, who trusted his fate to the arms of Baby Jesus. Yet, by instinct and experience, he knew luck had seldom walked the same field as him before and suspicioned it had something to do with his scarecrow. Not that it was magic or something un-Christian; it was more like a lucky penny.

Yet, his son knew different. He would look out from his bedroom window, late at night, watching the horrible thing twist and sway as if dancing in the moonlight. Sometimes, if the post hung bare, he would silently crawl back into his bed and shiver under the quilt, listening for footsteps creeping through the corn. There was one thing certain sure: whatever else was in that scarecrow – Baby Jesus had nothing to do with it.

But, there was another thing to keep him thinking. Whatever walked into that field – feathered or on four legs, with a mind to steal the corn – came to a bad end. It was well protected. Yet, towards what end and to what purpose?

What would happen when it came time to cut and gather the corn?

***

That day was soon coming. Joe Junior watched the hot evening grow chill, the blue summer sky being replaced by gloomy storm clouds the color of unbleached wool. Autumn winds came to churn the yellowed tops, the fields waving like gusts on troubled waters. JJ stood at the far edge of the field, his face pale and troubled. If he had dared, he would have set a match to it and watched it burn.

Then came the October morning when his Pa set him to sharpening the corn knives while he and the hired men put the Thresher in order and set it to hitch behind the mule team. Mist blanketed the low places; the corn rows rising up from it in ranks of rattling, skeletal fingers, caught in banks of boiling milk. By first light, all was ready and the men shouldered their glittering blades and waded into the corn.

And against all his wishes, Joe Junior re-entered the corn, as well. In this, Pa was standing no nonsense. He was spending money on hired men's wages, with the bank loans waiting to be paid by the crop. No foolish notions would keep his boy from doing his share. So, JJ reluctantly took the reins, guiding the thresher down the rows, laid bare by the swath of the corn knives. In his mind, he all but heard the cut stalks scream.

By noon, they had cleared several acres; fields flattened and the corn gathered in the hopper, like the loot of a conquering army. Pa called a rest, the men breaking out the cold chicken, biscuits and lemonade Mrs. Tobbers had set in the basket. Joe Junior left his untouched, making a pretense of watering the mules and picking the clumps of dirt from their shoes. He kept his eyes on the ground, not wishing to look up.

They rested in the middle of the field, Pa and the men sitting right in the shadow of the scarecrow post. It hung there, above them, twisting this way and that in the autumn wind, like a hanged man on a gallows. Its meal-sack head had settled some on the cross frame. It sagged wearily, bottle cap eyes hidden by its hat brim and it had lost its toothy smile. Two of the threads had rotted away from the corners, their caps dropping away, so that it had turned to a rotted-toothed grimace.

Just for an instant, when the men had been stooped over, swinging their corn knives, that head had swiveled on its wooden shoulders and stared straight at Joe Junior. It had lasted only a second, but there was no mistaking the cold accusation in the glance. Then it had swung away.

Joe hadn't dared look at it again.

An hour before sundown, Pa called a halt, proclaiming it a good day's work, and sending the men off with their wages in their pockets. It was Saturday night and he had promised his Missus to drive her into town to help plan the after services social at the church for the following day. There was still a bit of light in the sky as Joe Junior watched his parents drive off in the old Model T, raising a cloud of red dust behind.

***

He sat in his Daddy's chair, there on the porch, as the shadows stole across the flattened portions of the fields and the last of the sun burned orange on the horizon. Stars had begun to wink in a blue-black sky and the moon was a frosty patch of silver, rising up from the pine thickets.

Joe sat, rocking, watching – waiting. His eyes never left the post and the shadowed figure attached there. Stripped of the surrounding corn, it stood naked – a horrible, crucified idol or effigy from another time. The moonlight highlighted the brim of the hat, the outstretched arms. The tatters of its coat flapped like bats behind an abandoned church steeple.

If it was going to happen, it would come soon. He'd been thinking on this all summer. It took some of the scare out of it, but not much. He was glad his folks had left. It made it some easier to do what he had to, but the tension was awful – the night getting on.

It got chill, wind picking up and blowing clouds in from the east. They ringed the moon and the dark ran over the fields, like it would if he'd snuffed a lamp wick. Joe Junior got up, went inside. He sat at the kitchen table, in the silent house, still as a mouse with the cat dozing in the corner.

It was a small sound – the hint of a creak on the rotted porch steps, followed by the slow, dragging sweep of something moving on the porch itself. It was the same sound his Ma made when she broomed the clumps of dirt Pa's boots always left in the doorway. There was a faded lace curtain pulled over the window. There, in the darkness, Joe Junior watched the silhouette pass. It paused at the door.

There was a knock.

Joe slowly moved his hand towards the pocket of his overalls, feeling for the bundle of Diamond Strike Anywhere matches he'd been carrying there. There was a good fistful of them – almost the whole box – and he'd taped them tight together.

The knock repeated. The door rattled in its jamb and the brass knob jiggled against the catch.

Joe rose up, his heart in his mouth, and tip-toed his way to the door. He hesitated, breath catching in his throat, heart beating so fast, it was a drum in his ears. He forced his left hand to lie on the catch. His right hand clutched the fistful of matches, poised to strike the rough jamb of the door.

He prayed the straw wasn't wet.

He flung the door open and the same time, the matches flared, in an explosion of blinding light and flame.

Filling the door's frame, that horrible vision of straw, rags and malice stood outlined; the fire reflected in his bottle cap eyes, flickering off the corn knife clutched in the gloved hand. It took one, lurching step forward – right into the handful of burning matches that Joe thrust at its head.

There was the sputter and hiss of sparks catching, the acrid smoke-smell of old straw going up, and then the roar of racing fire as it swallowed its fuel. Yet, even enveloped in leaping flames, it shambled forward – disintegrating into glowing cinder and ash, but still animated by whatever power lay behind death and the grave.

The threadbare carpet was alive with sparks, the laced curtains scorched, before Joe could shake himself from the unreality of it. The thing was fixing to burn down the house. He took up a chair, pushed the flaming pile of rag and straw out on the porch – kicked it down the steps. He watched it squirm and twist, trying to claw itself across the yard, leaving a trail of blackened straw and ash. Joe followed, until it was no more than a vaguely man-shaped pile of soot.

He squatted beside it, watching – spreading it out with the tines of his rake. He was still there when, well after 10:00 p.m., his Daddy and Ma pulled into the driveway, and noticed the door open to the house; smelt burned carpet and saw their boy sitting out in the yard.

"Boy!" Joe heard the car door slam, his Daddy calling from across the drive. "What's amiss? You all right?"

"Yes, Daddy."

Joe Senior couldn't see the ghastly look on his boy's face – the haunted eyes and the deadly pallor. Yet, he couldn't miss the weary, empty tone of his son's voice.

"I'm all right. It's all fine, now."

Not until he looked up to face his Daddy, did Joe Senior get some notion of just how wrong things actually were. And he could make no sense of what the boy said, before his son collapsed in his arms.

"Daddy, I don't want to grow corn, no more. Let's, next year, put in cotton. We don't need a scarecrow for cotton, do we? I'm right tired of 'em."

ABOUT THE AUTHORS

Joseph Rubas is the author of over 200 short stories. His fiction has appeared in: Nameless Digest, The Storyteller, All Due Respect, Thuglit, The Horror Zine, and many others. He currently resides in Florida with his family.

Ken MacGregor's work has appeared in dozens of anthologies and magazines. His story collection, "An Aberrant Mind" is available online and in select bookstores. Ken is a member of the Great Lakes Association of Horror Writers and an Affiliate member of HWA. He edits an annual horror-themed anthology for the former. He has also dabbled in TV, radio, movies and sketch comedy. Oh, and movies. He made a horror movie. Nobody was killed. Really. Recently, he co-wrote a novel and is working on the sequel. Ken lives in Michigan with his family and two "domesticated" predators.
Website: http://ken-macgregor.com, Twitter: @kenmacgregor, Facebook:
https://www.facebook.com/KenMacGregorAuthor?ref=hl

Gillian French holds a BA in English from the University of Maine, Orono. Her short fiction can be found in Odd Tree Press's forthcoming Quarterly Publication, Sanitarium Magazine, and The Realm Beyond. Her fiction contest wins include Second Place in the Genre Short Story category of the 2013 Annual Writer's Digest Writing Competition, First Place in the Horror category of the 2012 Writer's Digest Popular Fiction Awards Competition, and Third Prize in the 2012 Zoetrope: All-Story Short Fiction Contest. She lives in rural Maine with her husband Darren and their son Jeremy. Haunt her at
www.gillianfrench.wordpress.com.

About the Authors

Jay Seate is the winner of Horror Novel Review's 2013 Best Short Fiction Award. He writes everything from humor to the erotic to the macabre, and is especially keen on transcending genre pigeonholing. Over two hundred stories appear in magazines, anthologies and webzines. They may be told with hardcore realism or humor, bringing to life the most unlovely of characters. See longer works at www.melange-books.com and www.museituppublishing.com for those who like tales intertwined with the paranormal.
Website: www.troyseateauthor.webs.com.

Ellen Denton is a freelance writer living in the Rocky Mountains with her husband and two demonic cats who wreak havoc and hell (the cats, not the husband). She's had an exciting life working as a circus acrobat, a CIA spy, a service provider in the Red Light District, a navy seal, a ballerina on the starship Enterprise, and was the first person to ever climb Mount Everest. (Editorial note: Some of the above may be fictional.)

Adrian Ludens is a radio announcer and short story author from Rapid City, South Dakota. His collection, *When Bedbugs Bite*, is available from Amazon, Barnes & Noble and other sites in a variety of formats, including Kindle. Other recent and upcoming anthology appearances include: Shadows Over Main Street (Hazardous Press), Surreal Worlds (Bizarro Pulp Press), The Gothic Fantasy Book of Science Fiction (Flame Tree Publishing) and The Mammoth Book of Jack the Ripper Stories (Little, Brown). He is an Active member of the Horror Writers Association. Adrian is a fan of hockey, heavy metal, and horror fiction, and enjoys exploring abandoned buildings. Visit www.adrianludens.com.

Kris Ashton is an Australian author best known for his tales of horror and dark speculative fiction. His short stories have appeared in *Perihelion SF*, *Midnight Echo*, *Andromeda Spaceways*, and *Dark Moon Digest*, while his third novel, *Invasion at Bald Eagle*, was released earlier this year. Kris is also a noted journalist and has worked as a film critic, book reviewer and travel writer. He lives in Sydney with his wife, daughter and a slightly mad boxer dog. He keeps a website full of book and movie reviews, essays about writing, personal anecdotes, and the 'stories behind his stories' (including how he conceived 'Night Feeds'). You'll find all that, along with links to his Facebook page and Twitter account, at **kris-ashton.wix.com/spec-fic**.

Ken Goldman, former Philadelphia teacher of English and Film Studies, is an affiliate member of the Horror Writers Association. He has homes on the Main Line in Pennsylvania and at the Jersey shore (where during the summer months, like the 50-something Arthur Fitz of "Buy...Psyche...Kill," Ken bikes the length of the Atlantic City boardwalk several times a week, watching the crazies and seeking inspiration for his tales). Ken drives a midlife crisis red Corvette, and, yes ladies, he's single (and everyone knows how attractive horror writers are to women.) His stories have appeared in over 765 independent press publications in the U.S., Canada, the UK, and Australia with over forty due for upcoming publication in 2015-2016. Since 1993 Ken's tales have received seven honorable mentions in The Year's Best Fantasy & Horror. He has written five books, including three anthologies of short stories, titled: *You Had Me At Arrgh!!* (Sam's Dot Publishers), *Donny Doesn't Live Here Anymore* (A/A Productions), and *Star-Crossed* (Vampires 2); and a novella, *Desiree*, (Damnation Books). His first novel, *Of A Feather* (Horrific Tales Publishing), was released in January 2014.

Ken requests you hold your applause until the royalty checks arrive. But enough about me -- no, wait, there's more... Check out stories and other goodies by Ken Goldman here. He can be found on Amazon's Author Central. Bring money:

http://www.facebook.com/kenneth.goldman1

and: https://www.goodreads.com/Goldman

and: https://plus.google.com/110939908295908428356/posts.

Louis Rakovich writes sometimes-fantastical literary fiction. His short stories have appeared in *Bartleby Snopes*, *The Fiction Desk*, *Criminal Element*, *Goldfish Grimm*, *Phobos Magazine* and other places. He's inspired by authors such as Truman Capote, Gabriel Garcia Marquez and Edgar Poe, and filmmakers such as David Lynch and Andrei Tarkovsky. He grew up in Jerusalem, Israel, and currently lives in NYC, where he's working on his first novel – a psychological thriller with theological undertones. You can find more stories by him at www.louisrakovich.com, or follow him on Twitter @LouisRakovich.

James Coplin grew up on spooky stories; EC Comics, Monsters of Film Land Magazines, Eerie, Creepy, Edgar Allan Poe. When he got home from school his fingers couldn't hit the dial fast enough to turn on the Four O'clock Creature Features and at night he would watch Boris Karloff's Thriller, Sebastian Cabot's Ghost Stories, Twilight Zone and Outer Limits. His parents worried about him. He still likes a good, basic fright story – atmosphere, all the shared nervousness of being left in the dark in an unfamiliar place – and then hearing the creak of floorboards above. I mean, ghosts can't really hurt you, right? –Are you sure?

Josh Shiben lives in the swamps of Fredericksburg, Virginia with his wife and two mongrels. An aerospace engineer by day and couch potato by night, Josh has, from a young age, been in love with storytelling. Whether they be told through published works, e-books, or simply around a burning campfire, he's always particularly loved the captivating, yet intimate power of a scary story. Born in the late eighties, Josh spent his formative years reading Goosebumps, watching Are You Afraid of the Dark, and hiding under the blankets reading the esteemed Alan Schwartz's *Scary Stories to Tell in the Dark*. Today, his favorite authors include Dan Simmons, Stephen King, Richard Matheson and H.P. Lovecraft. His first novella, *Dreams of Eschaton*, is available now on amazon. He also blogs (ir)regularly at: PoetMoreate.blogspot.com.

Mike Thorn recently completed his Honours B.A. in English at Mount Royal University, and he is currently pursuing his M.A. in English at the University of Calgary. His poetry and prose has been published in the campus press *STOPGap*, and his essay "The Relocation of Monstrosity: An Analysis of Horror in Brian De Palma's *Carrie*" was published in *Mount Royal Undergraduate Humanities Review*. He has several mirrors in his home, which he uses regularly. He hasn't yet seen anything more terrifying than his own reflection in the midst of exam week.

Kerry G.S. Lipp lives in Louisville, Kentucky. He hates the sun and loves making fun of dead people. His parents started reading his stories and they've consequently booted him from their will. Kerry's work appears in several anthologies including *DOA2* from Blood Bound Books. He's become a regular on The Wicked Library podcast. He is currently editing his first novel, writing his second, and shopping a bizarro novella. Kerry rarely (but still) blogs at www.HorrorTree.com and will launch his own website sometime before he dies. Say hi on Twitter @kerrylipp or come find him on Facebook. And he wants you to remember to always cover the camera on your laptop. You never know who is watching you.

Robert Essig is the author of the novels *In Black*, *People of the Ethereal Realm* and *Through the In Between, Hell Awaits*. He has also published over sixty short stories and two novellas. Robert is a member of the HWA. He lives with his family in Southern California.

Jack Bantry is the editor of Splatterpunk Zine. He works as a postman and resides in a small town at the edge of the North York Moors.

Adam Millard is the author of twenty novels, ten novellas, and more than a hundred short stories, which can be found in various collections and anthologies. Probably best known for his post-apocalyptic fiction, Adam also writes fantasy/horror for children, as well as bizarro fiction for several publishers. His "Dead" series has been the filling in a Stephen King/Bram Stoker sandwich on Amazon's bestsellers chart, and the translation rights have recently sold to German publisher, Voodoo Press.
www.adammillard.co.uk
Facebook: https://www.facebook.com/Adam.L.Millard
Twitter: @adammillard
Sign up to receive Adam's monthly newsletter:
www.adammillard.co.uk/newsletter.html
Wikipedia: https://en.wikipedia.org/wiki/Adam_Millard

This is **Bernard McGhee**'s first fiction publication. But when not collecting rejection letters, he works the overnight desk in a busy newsroom, which provides a constant source of inspiration for writing horror stories. He was raised in the New Orleans area but has lived all around the country and currently lives in Atlanta with his wife and son. You can follow him on Twitter @BMcGhee13.

D.M. Kayahara resides in Winnipeg, Manitoba, Canada. She writes stories for fun and thinks you should too.

Gerry Huntman is a writer based in Melbourne, Australia, living with his wife and young daughter. He writes in all genres - and most sub-genres - of speculative fiction, although his stories tend toward dark. He has sold over 50 short pieces of fiction, the more recent in the professional market. He has been included in Ticonderoga Publishing's 2014 edition of the Best Australian Fantasy and Horror anthology, to be published in late 2015. He recently published a young teen fantasy novel, Guardian of the Sky Realms (Cohesion Press, 2014). He is also the Managing Director and Chief Editor of IFWG Publishing, a small, independent speculative fiction company.

Blog Site: http://gerryhuntman.livejournal.com

Ed Ahern resumed writing after forty odd years in foreign intelligence and international sales. He's had over eighty stories and poems published thus far, as well as his collected fairy and folk tales, "The Witch Made Me Do It," and a mystery/horror novella "The Witches' Bane." He's reachable on Facebook, Twitter @bottomstripper or on his web site: www.swampgasworks.com

Ed has his original wife, but advises that after forty-seven years they are both out of warranty. Their (usual superlatives) two children and five grandchildren live too far away from Connecticut. Ed's lived in five countries and visited almost eighty. He speaks pretty good German and French and pretty bad Japanese. Ed dissipates his free time fly fishing and shooting.